THE GAME OF LIFE

BARBARA BOOTH

BOSUN

BOOKS

Copyright © Barbara Booth 2000

All rights reserved

No part of this book may be reproduced by any means, nor transmitted, nor translated into a machine language, without the written permission of the publisher.

Bosun Books
11 Lyndhurst Road
Chichester
West Sussex
PO19 2LF

A CIP catalogue record for this book is available from the British Library.

Printed and bound in Great Britain

ISBN 0 9537694 0 2

Cover design Ron Sandford

About the Author

Barbara Booth was born in Spain. After a short period of nursing and a happy three years with a family in Washington DC, she worked her way round the world, and after several years of likely and unlikely temporary jobs, including marriage, she settled down to constituency work for MPs at the House of Commons, and a pre-retirement year working for Norma Major at 10 Downing Street. During this time she gained a BA Honours degree at the Open University, a Post Graduate Certificate in Education and a Diploma in Dyslexia Therapy. In retirement she paints miniatures (exhibiting regularly), gives occasional help to children suffering from dyslexia, and works at the local hospice. She has published short stories and articles. This is her first novel.

One

Marjorie sat straight-backed, close to the bed where her father was considering his last moments on earth. Colonel Passley knew his daughters were there. Marjorie on one side, Molly on the other. He was ready to go, but he wanted no fuss. Marjorie would see to that. He opened his eyes and slowly turned his head towards her. She was making a list as she sat there - a list, no doubt, of what Molly would have to do as soon as he had gone. The old soldier approved. Even as you were going into action the commanding officer had to be thinking ahead, deploying his troops. His troops? Her troops? Could one person be a troop? He was too tired to work it out. All he knew was that she would do the right thing. Always had.

She looked up and gave him a nod of greeting. 'Father?'

His eyes closed, then suddenly they opened again, as if in surprise. There was a pause, then 'Thank you' he whispered, and closed his eyes for ever.

Marjorie almost smiled in acknowledgement. It was good to be appreciated, and mostly she had been. She was the rôle model for Molly, younger by three years. She had read about rôle models in a magazine at the dentist recently. Yes, that was just what she was and had been to them all. These pleasant thoughts were interrupted as Molly, eyes red-rimmed, her agitated hands clutching her damp handkerchief, gasped 'Is he - ? Oh, Marjorie, has he - ?'

Marjorie leaned forward and touched the old man's hand. 'He's gone, Molly,' she said, matter-of-factly, and Molly laid her head on the bed and sobbed.

Marjorie twitched the sheet straight and removed a crease from the coverlet. 'Now, Molly, come along dear. It was expected and it was easy. Look at him Molly, he's at peace.' And with a rare flash of imagination she added 'He has gone to join mother - you couldn't grudge him that.'

Molly raised her head and for a moment her grief was held in abeyance as she gazed at her father's face. Apart from a pinched look around his nose his face was serene. The lines of tension had vanished and before them, gentle in clean blue-striped pyjamas, lay the strong man of their youth, with age stripped from him. His dignity was intact. She dabbed her eyes with her handkerchief, laid her hand for a moment on his, and got to her feet. She looked at Marjorie questioningly.

'Go and make a pot of tea,' Marjorie said, and Molly gratefully left the room.

Marjorie made sure everything was tidy, that he was tidy. She pulled the curtains across the three large windows, the big wooden curtain rings sounding very final as they swished along their rails. Leaving the room she pulled the door to, but did not close it. They would not leave him quite alone.

Molly heard her coming downstairs, going to the telephone to ring the doctor. Marjorie was so right, she thought. As ever. Of course it would be selfish to grudge him his reunion and his peace. And after all, this time Marjorie had been there.

Molly remembered the shock of their mother's death. No-one had expected it to happen so suddenly. She had been in bed for a week, a chill had turned to pneumonia, but the doctor seemed pleased with her progress. Marjorie had gone to her room for a rest. Then suddenly, whilst Molly was trying to coax her mother with a little soup, she had opened her eyes wide, looked questioningly over Molly's shoulder, and died. She had wanted to check with Marjorie, but Marjorie wasn't there. It seemed wrong, and Molly felt that their mother would have died easier in her mind if Marjorie had indicated that the end was near.

Colonel Passley had accepted his loss with fortitude. He had thought he might go before his wife and he was glad not to have deserted her again, as he had had to during the war.

In 1940 John Passley had married a girl he met in the blackout. Jessica had been waiting in Sloane Square for a bus to take her to World's End, where she shared a flat with two other girls with whom she worked at the Censorship. John was waiting for a bus to Putney Bridge. After half an hour, and a few comments on the bus service war or no war, John tentatively suggested having a drink at the pub on the corner. Squeezing their way through blackout curtains into a well-lit bar they looked at each other and liked what they saw. It was always possible to imagine someone was attractive when you could only hear a voice, so that the fact that Jessica was slim and pretty, with brown hair and expressive eyes, and John was a good looking blue-eyed officer, was to each a pleasant surprise.

Jessica was twenty-five and John nearly thirty. Because of their happiness together they looked much younger, and to the Passleys they were the ideal young couple.

John would leave Jessica at Waterloo on his way back to camp feeling like a teenager. Reaching camp and seeing soldiers not yet twenty he found it hard to believe he was the same person. They were married quietly, two months after that first meeting.

When he was at home, which was fairly often at first, he and Jessica would take the District Line into the West End where they danced the whole night through. They loved to sit in Green Park as dawn broke, have coffee at Lyons Corner House, and take the first bus back to Putney, where they lived with John's parents. It was not the time to find a home of their own and Jessica felt they were the parents she had never had - close, loving, always concerned.

Once the bombing started John's parents worried about them when they were out all night, but they said they were careful and went to shelters whenever the sirens raised the alarm. In fact they never did, feeling as if they had special dispensation from the gods. Sometimes their journey home took twice as long as previously, the bus making detours to avoid bomb craters. Everyone on the bus would have some story either of how they would have been blown up if they hadn't decided to do something different to their usual routine; or having been bombed out several times. There was sympathy for those who had suffered but a feeling that, as in all matters of life and death, it was not likely to happen to them. Until it did, and then they often knew nothing about it.

Walking up Putney Hill and along Wimbledon Common on a beautiful spring or summer morning, passing fences over which the honeysuckle sprawled, scenting the air, was something completely outside war and death. It was eternal. In later life they avoided honeysuckle, as they avoided certain tunes, which would fill them with a devastating sense of loss. Those days could never be recaptured.

Knowing that John would be sent abroad one day they were eager to have a baby and after two years, when they had begun to wonder if it would ever happen, Jessica felt signs of life within her. Their happiness was complete. And it was at this moment of supreme happiness that John was posted overseas. He could not tell her where he was going and when they parted at Waterloo he joked and said it was probably the north of England and he'd be home on leave in a week or two. She had almost believed him, and became frantic when no letters came. She wrote to the War Office and they assured her all was well. There was no way troops could communicate on long sea voyages. The day the first letter arrived should have been one of pure joy, and the sight of the envelope brought tears of relief to her eyes, but when she saw it was from Singapore her heart turned over. Singapore had fallen to the Japanese the previous day.

The Passleys and Jessica kept each other's spirits up and waited for news. Mrs Passley saw it as her duty to keep Jessica well fed and she spent hours in queues collecting their rations and extras which suddenly became available. The Censorship was in central London and Jessica's journeys home were often hazardous, but it was a time of closeness and you were never alone. Everyone knew what they were doing and why and everyone had some heavy load to bear. Together they could overcome crises and problems which three years before would have reduced most of them to a state of nervous collapse.

Six weeks before the baby was due Jessica left the Censorship. Her blood pressure was up and she must rest. There was still no news of John and it was hard for her to pretend to his parents that she did not often wonder whether they would ever hear from him again.

On the morning of her final spell of night duty Jessica walked up Putney Hill and, smelling the honeysuckle, her spirits rose. She felt all would be well. Somehow John would survive. Smiling to herself, feeling the baby gently kicking, she wandered slowly up the hill and along by Wimbledon Common. The war would soon be over and John would be home, and they would be three.

Suddenly she noticed a pall of smoke ahead of her. It must be very close to the Passley's block of flats. She started to run. There were ambulances, a fire engine, and soon she was climbing over coils of hoses. The block of flats was a shambles. 'Steady there,' said a fireman, rushing forward to catch her. In front of this ghastly mayhem Jessica collapsed.

Some days later she came to in Putney Hospital. Looking out of the window she saw the trees, heard the birds, and remembered everything. She felt her stomach. It was flat. 'The baby,' she whispered, and a voice at her side said 'It's all right, she's not far away. I'll tell Sister you've come round. I won't be a tick.' A young Red Cross nurse had jumped up from the stool on which she had been sitting beside Jessica's bed and hurried out of the room.

The Sister was amazed to find that Jessica remembered the moment she fell to the ground. Etched on her memory was the devastation of the block of flats and, weirdly sticking out of a part of the smoking rubble, the twisted remains of the pram she had been given only a week before by someone living in one of the ground floor flats.

Before she asked the question she knew the answer. 'Are they dead?'

'I'm afraid so, my dear. There was only one survivor. An old lady in the basement flat.'

'She wouldn't allow anyone to take shelter in her flat,' said Jessica sadly.

The Sister shook her head. 'That's life,' she said.

But of course it wasn't, it was death to all those who lived in the block. All except one old lady.

They brought the baby to her but she couldn't feel anything. All she knew was that because of her marrying John his parents had been killed. They had only stayed in London to make a home for John and Jessica.

A week later there was a telegram from the War Office. 'I hope you don't mind,' said the Sister. 'I opened it. It's all right. It's good news.'

John had got out of Singapore. She would be hearing from him soon. If only his parents had known. Perhaps they did know. All emotion had drained out of her and Jessica no longer felt that the most important thing in the world was to hear from John. She tried to get a message to him about his parents and about the baby, and the War Office promised to do their best, but now it was up to her to decide what to do next. When John's aunt in Sutherland said she and the baby must come to Scotland and stay with her until John came home this seemed the best solution. Jessica had no near relatives in Britain. She had never been close to her parents and in 1938, when war began to look inevitable, they had gone to Australia. Her father had been offered a job at a branch of his firm in Sydney. Not only was it promotion but he saw it as an escape from his increasingly difficult wife. But she saw it as an opportunity to get away from the prospect of war, bombs, invasion even. To Jessica she said casually 'You'll want to be in the thick of it. It's your generation's war after all.' The firm assumed they would be going as a couple, there would be entertaining to take care of, and passages were booked for them without question. So, in a state of armed truce, they left. To Jessica it was no personal loss. They had never been interested in her. They had wanted a boy. In fact she was relieved to see them go, and apart from Christmas cards, signed only by her mother, she heard no more from them. Whether they had parted, as was very likely, or her father had died, she never knew. When she and John decided to get married John insisted she should write and tell her mother. She wrote care of her father's firm, the only address she had, but all she received in reply was a cable 'Hope you'll have better luck than I did.' John was shocked but Jessica laughed. 'Typical,' was all she said.

Even if her mother had been able or willing to come over from Australia now Jessica knew she would be no comfort at all.

She had been given an address to write to John, mostly numbers and capital letters, and she told him about his parents and that the baby had been born. She would call her Marjorie after his mother. The feeling that the letter might never reach him, and her acquaintance with the Censorship, inhibited her and she wrote a rather stilted letter. She said she was taking Marjorie up to

Sutherland and reminded him of the address. That was all she could do.

Aunt Jane was an austere lady and Marjorie, even when a baby, seemed to have a similar character. Here nature and nurture were in complete accord and when, after a year, Jessica started to work at a nearby hospital she would return to find Jane and Marjorie sitting together most companionably. Marjorie was a good baby, and as soon as she started to walk she followed Aunt Jane about and tried to do whatever her great-aunt did. When the time came for looking at books Marjorie took this very seriously and she and Aunt Jane studied Rupert Bear as if it were a textbook on ethics. Some characters were 'good' and others 'bad', and there was nothing in between. Marjorie's stubby finger would point and she would say 'bad'. 'Indeed,' Aunt Jane would agree. But when Rupert was depicted taking a basket of goodies to his grandmother it was 'good', and 'yes, very good'.

Marjorie was certainly not a child for cuddling, and Jessica found she didn't mind. They liked each other, and even respected each other, but somehow Marjorie was not a symbol of her love for John but of the change in her life from innocence to guilt.

By now she had heard from the War Office that John was fighting in the jungle. He couldn't write but she would receive messages each month from the War Office on his behalf. These invariably said 'Fit and well, love, John.'

The 'fit and well' messages continued until Jessica wondered whether this was just a cover for the fact that he was dead, and that all wives received them so that morale on the home front would keep going.

However one day she arrived back at the house to find a telegram. She felt immediately that it held bad news and even Aunt Jane advised her to sit down before opening it. Marjorie solemnly watched her mother's face. All three of them sat down at the kitchen table, on which a pot of tea (for shock) was already standing. Jessica opened the telegram with trembling fingers and read out 'Am in India. Fit and well. Writing. John.' Ironically the real John sent no love.

He was in fact far from fit and well, and after eighteen months working at Military HQ in Karachi he was shipped home.

But it had never been the same. He and Jessica had grown apart. The first serious, formative happenings had come too late in their lives, and each had had to cope alone. If John had been younger he might have been more resilient, but his gloom pervaded their lives. They came together again deeply scarred and neither knew how to attempt to bridge the gap which lay between them. Each felt in some way let down by the other, yet could not face the fact. John never spoke directly of his parents' death, or of the trauma through which Jessica must have passed, and she never referred to it. But neither did he speak of his experiences in the Far East and she could not bring herself to ask him about them. What had seemed so wonderful at the start, their very alikeness, was now the stumbling block, and there was no older generation to advise or interfere, which would have brought them closer, and they felt that they were the older generation.

John's love making was dutifully performed, but there was no ardour, no moment when Jessica felt he and she were one being, no ecstasy. Perhaps this was the inevitable progress of married life, she thought, and she took what comfort she could from it. They were older. They were together. It was good to have him there beside her, to know that if she hugged him he would hug her back, but it was depressing to be aware that he remained within himself, whatever he did was as routine as breathing or walking. It was as though he regarded sex as part of a sensibly healthy regime. Thinking back to those days when they had lain in bed together, happily exhausted, reluctant to get up and face the dreary humdrum day, she could hardly believe John was the same man. If she asked him now 'Do you love me?' he would reply 'Of course,' before turning on his side and falling asleep. He never had nightmares, or tossed and turned, when she could have kissed him awake and shared his torment. As with everything in his life now, it all held the same level of importance. Sleeping, breathing, eating, making love, working. He was not the man she married. But neither was she that woman.

They bought a house in Bournemouth, from which John commuted daily to and from the War Office, and it was here that Molly was born, the day after the war in Europe ended. Jessica felt this should be a reason for optimism, but the sight and sound of the celebrations for victory in Europe threw John into deeper despair. His friends in the Far East were still in danger, and how many of them would get home? How many of their wives would have the chance of mothering their children? Why should he not only be home, but be a father again?

He took a week off to look after Marjorie. Her primness suited him perfectly and he spoke to her as to an adult. Neither of them expressed more than academic interest in the new baby, even when they first saw her, and Jessica, after a difficult delivery, was too tired to care. They collected mother and child at the end of the week and on the way home Marjorie said 'I 'spect you'll call her Jane - like Aunt Jane.' But Jessica was firm. She was to be called Molly, after her own mother. Molly would be the kind of person she wished her mother had been.

As Molly grew into a little girl Jessica realised that she was by nature very unlike either her mother or John's aunt. She was gentle and unselfish, and Marjorie's disinterest changed as the baby grew and she found her the ideal foil for her own bossiness. Molly could not have been more satisfactory had she been ordered from Harrods.

Jessica found she was perfectly content to stay at home with the children. She read a little, mostly autobiographies and biographies, from which she learned that not many people seemed to achieve very fulfilled personal lives, which was a comfort. And she knitted. She never minded how often she had to unravel jerseys which Marjorie found too tight round the neck or sleeve, or socks which John complained were too short or too long. Her horizons, never very wide, became ever more limited.

When John was fifty he was retired from the army on health grounds, and on medical advice they took the dramatic step of going on a cruise to the Pacific islands. They disliked the heat, the noise and the people and although the children seemed to enjoy themselves in their quiet way it was not a success. John had become an old man before his time. Back in Bournemouth they moved to a large Victorian house called Balmoral, in Upper Park Drive, where they could keep themselves to themselves.

John expressed an interest in military history and spent many hours in the library, or his study, doing 'research'. He spoke of writing a book one day. The family never inquired about it, and he would escape from them with the words 'I'm going to do some research'. This came more and more to mean only that he was going into his study and did not wish to be disturbed.

The girls were brought up to be self-sufficient and they appeared content. Marjorie always took the lead. She arranged all their holiday activities - asked their mother to pack tea, and under Marjorie's supervision Molly would carry it to the appointed spot. If the tide came in too soon, or it started to rain, Marjorie would climb the rocks and direct operations from above, get on the one bicycle and pedal swiftly home, to keep it from getting wet and rusting up. She was always so thoughtful. When they were older Marjorie sent Molly to get tickets for the Bournemouth Symphony Orchestra, or the theatre. For a while after leaving school they would make up parties with friends, but as the years went by the friends got married and drifted away. They continued to go on occasion to the highly respectable Abbey Ball Rooms, where, without advice, Molly had to make up her own mind whether to accept an invitation to dance or, more alarmingly, to sit out on the balcony. But eventually these outings became rarer, until they were no more.

John kept a Morris Minor in the garage. He often viewed it but seldom used it after he retired, and Marjorie decided to learn to drive. Despite going over a red light and blaming all and sundry for her near misses the Inspector, impressed by her imperious manner, passed her. Unfortunately, before she had time to work out scenic routes along which to transport her admiring family, there was an accident. 'Stupid man, came out of a turning and hit me,' she said indignantly. Her mother and Molly were equally indignant, and even her father, whose pride and joy the Morris Minor was, sympathised. 'Not enough to be a good driver. Got to watch out for the bad ones,' he said.

Despite the indignity of a police interview (and how could her age possibly throw any light on the state of mind of the idiot who had hit her?) the insurance company insisted on a detailed claim. 'Surely they can accept my word for it,' snorted Marjorie, and was only slightly mollified when her father explained that it was routine. But worse was to follow. The dreadful man involved in the accident insisted that *she* had hit him, and the insurance investigator said that the direction of the impact confirmed this.

Marjorie was furious. 'It's all very well writing things down, anyone can do that. If I could just see these people face to face I'm sure I could sort it all out. It's a disgrace. I'll sue them.' However she was deterred by her father who said it would only make a small affair bigger. 'And you know what the papers are,' added her mother. Indeed she did. A spotty-faced youth had come round the previous week to ask her about the accident. 'I understand from a witness the two cars moved along side by side for a while. Like a dance, he said. Very clever. Wish I'd seen it. What's the story?'

He was turned smartly away from the door but this did not stunt his imagination.

On an inside page of the local paper was the headline 'Dancing Cheek to Cheek', and below 'Miss Marjorie Passley, aged 28, danced cheek to cheek with Mr Henry Humphries, aged 56. Witness Mr John Hargreaves, aged 51, said he'd never seen anything like it. He was walking along ...' Marjorie had been beside herself. 'Horrible young man - all of seventeen-and-a-half I'm sure. How dare he.'

As her parents said, best to leave it at that. *They* knew the truth and that's all that mattered. After which Marjorie never drove again. 'Why bother?' she said. 'I've always enjoyed trains and buses - we all have,' and she eyed her family severely. They chorused their agreement, and her father was only too glad to have his treasure back in the garage.

Marjorie and Molly attended various classes over the years but eventually their enthusiasm waned. Marjorie was inclined to choose a lecture-based course, which usually led to disagreements with the lecturers. Molly chose more practical outlets, but if she did create a pot or hang up a painting to dry, by the following week someone would have knocked the one or brushed up against the other, and it was too disappointing. She preferred to do embroidery at home.

Imperceptibly, their youth slipped away. Half-hearted stabs at romance, no more than a fumbled kiss on the doorstep, hands held in the cinema, at least so far as Molly was concerned - all came to nothing. Whatever else Marjorie got up to, and she did have some unexplained outings, came to nothing either. 'The girls' drifted into early middle age almost without noticing it, and their parents became frail, subject to a variety of ailments well suited to the combined talents of the sisters. Whilst Marjorie organised things, Molly ran up and down stairs, hither and thither, in a whirl of activity.

Being looked after so well, having a settled routine and no worries, ensured a longer life than either Jessica or John would have wished for in their middle age, but they were, in their own ways, content.

After his wife died John Passley knew his daughters would take care of him, and in fact life would be easier in many ways. He would be their sole concern. And he had been, for five more years.

Now he was gone. Tears again filled Molly's eyes. It was hard to believe that both parents were dead, would never again speak, walk, hear, think or move, never call out, first with authority, later with advice, latterly for help. Their voices would never be heard again. The tears flowed as Molly realised that she could no longer remember the sound of her mother's voice.

Marjorie had finished on the phone. 'Molly, where's that tea?' She came swiftly into the kitchen. 'Come along, now. No good crying. That won't bring him back - kettle's boiling - make the tea - there are some biscuits left in the tin, aren't there? Bring the tray to the sitting room.' And she whirled out again, like someone organising a social event.

Molly pulled herself together - felt herself catching Marjorie's spirit. Straightening up she got the tea ready and brought it to her sister.

Marjorie was studying her list. 'Once he's been taken away - ' Molly choked on her biscuit - one of his favourite shortcake biscuits - 'Once the room is empty, we must clear everything up. I'll help you get the suitcases from the attic and while you do the packing I'll see to the funeral arrangements. You can strip the bed and leave it unmade. Open the windows.'

'But shouldn't we leave the curtains drawn?'

'That's old fashioned. No-one does it these days. No, the room needs airing, the furniture polishing. I noticed yesterday there's a mark on the bedside table. Try a little vinegar...' Marjorie continued, and after a while Molly stopped listening. She knew Marjorie would remind her of the rest.

She watched her with admiration. As striking looking at forty-eight as she had always been. Her fair hair, only faintly sprinkled with grey, was drawn tightly back and somehow pinned up. Now, with a quick, decisive and familiar movement, her hand touched the back of her head, ensuring that no pin had slipped out of place. Her firm mouth, lean face and grey eyes gave her the look of someone in authority, someone reliable.

Once a week a Mrs Turtle came in to do a thorough clean of the house. She was a lady after Marjorie's own heart. From the moment she arrived, and after they had exchanged views on the state of the weather, she set to, only stopping for a cup of tea and a sandwich at lunch time. Who but Marjorie could have found such a paragon? Molly wondered whether Mrs Turtle would still be needed, now there was no invalid in the house.

'Now Molly, you're day dreaming again. You'd better clear up the tea.' Marjorie's firm voice cut across Molly's thoughts.

The door bell rang and Marjorie said, 'That will be Dr Hill. Make a fresh pot for him, Molly dear.'

Molly scuttled away. Irreverently she thought that Marjorie's list must have read:

3 p.m. Father dies.

4 o'clock. Tea.

4.30 Dr Hill arrives.

4.45 More tea.

But that was a macabre, even cynical thought, and one so alien to Molly that she wondered whether she was having a breakdown, and immediately dismissed it from her mind.

Two

Their father's will brought no surprises. The house and money were to be shared between the sisters. There was no reason why they should change their lives in any way. On their outings Marjorie continued to walk a little ahead of Molly - or was it Molly walking a little behind Marjorie? Mr Whalley next door said to his wife 'There goes the royal family. On walkabout.'

'Hardly, dear,' said his wife. 'They talk to people on walkabouts.'

'Well the small plump one sort of bobs her head at people.'

The sisters passed from view. Mrs Whalley was right. They were somehow apart and aloof, for all Molly's vague smiles.

At the Indian paper shop the proprietor handed Marjorie the Daily Telegraph and said kindly to Molly 'Good morning Parsley.' 'Miss,' snapped Marjorie. 'Parsley Miss', he said, good naturedly, and Molly smiled and said 'Good morning.'

In the street Marjorie said 'Really, they are impossible. If he can't understand it's a surname at least he might *pronounce* it correctly. Parsley indeed! Why not mint or thyme?' and she snorted indignantly.

'Thyme would be nice,' said Molly thoughtfully, 'but then everyone would pronounce the "h" and that would spoil it.'

'Don't be absurd, Molly. Sometimes I wonder - '

'What dear?'

'Nothing. Now come along.'

They continued their rounds - butcher, baker, dairy, ending up in Claytons on the front for a cup of coffee. On the way home they passed a new estate agents. Marjorie stopped to look at prices. 'There's a house like ours going for £150,000 - I wonder what we would get for Balmoral?'

Molly was shocked. 'Sell Balmoral? Why? Oh Marjorie, we couldn't.'

'I didn't say we would sell, I just want to find out what it's worth. Come on Molly, I'm going to ask for someone to come round and give us an estimate.'

'But Marjorie - '

Two days later a man appeared at their front door and presented his card. Roy Bryce - Hacker and Hacker, Estate Agents. He was propelled briskly through the house by Marjorie, whilst Molly got the tea ready in the kitchen. She wondered whether she could, or even should, say to Marjorie 'It would be difficult to sell half a house.' But would Marjorie understand what she meant? She would probably just say 'Indeed it would', and Molly would say no more. It was always like that, mainly because Molly felt sure that Marjorie was bound to be right. But what had got into her? Could she really be thinking of moving? A bell tinkled in the sitting room and Molly set off with the tray.

Roy Bryce seemed a pleasant enough man. Fortyish, thin, glasses, darkish hair, greyish eyes. He was an 'ish' sort of man, neither quite one thing or another. Marjorie was at her most grand. 'Yes,' she was saying, 'My father bought that in India. He was there during the war. *Regular* Army - '

'Of course,' said Roy Bryce, impressed.

'This is my sister,' said Marjorie, indicating Molly's plump figure advancing on them with a tea tray. Molly smiled a rather worried smile.

'How d'you do, Miss Passley.' Roy Bryce surveyed the sisters calculatingly. Must be well off. Probably had friends in the same situation as themselves - rattling about in houses grown too big for them; some good pieces of furniture. He was seriously thinking of going into antiques on the side. He decided Marjorie was the one to cultivate. He told her that now was the time to sell. The bottom was about to fall out of the market. Inflation was rising again. Interest rates would go up.

Marjorie looked thoughtful and studied Mr Bryce as calculatingly as he had studied her. He seemed quite a clever young man; well, comparatively young. She really had no intention of persuading Molly to sell the house. She had just wanted some action. Now that there were no invalids in the house, no elders in any state of health in fact, to hang on her every word and do her bidding she felt a sense of frustration. Her talents were being wasted. If she weren't careful she would be reduced to joining the WI or the local Conservatives, and she suspected it would take months or even years to impress them with her abilities. She knew well how petty jealousies could intrude. People resented it if you were always right. She remembered this from her school days. Even when she ended up as head prefect there remained some girls who were ungrateful. This was the price one had to pay.

She had a little book beside her bed - *The Game of Life and How to Play It*. There had been a period some ten years back when her parents seemed to have lost their faith in her. Father had refused to wear a scarf for his walk along the front. Mother had refused to rest. One day they had suddenly said they were going for a weekend to Cheltenham on their own. A well-thumbed page in *The Game of Life* ... helped her over this. 'When people seem not to appreciate you, if they appear to rebuff you, remember, so long as you know you are doing your unselfish best for them, you can ignore their hurtful words and actions. Turn the other cheek. They will suffer most. We pass this way but once ...' and so on. And it was true. After a while her patience and persistence won them back, and they never made another bid for freedom.

Whilst going through their father's things they came across two old stamp albums. Molly thought the stamps very pretty and wanted to keep them but Marjorie decided to have them valued. One book contained Commonwealth stamps, quite a few triangular ones, some from the Cape of Good Hope, and the other book was dedicated to British Victorian stamps. The valuer was impressed and advised Marjorie to put them in an auction in two months' time, so they parted with the albums. Marjorie thought that if that sale went off well she might put one or two of the larger pieces of furniture in an auction.

Her cat-and-mouse game with Roy Bryce gave her enormous pleasure. Sometimes he thought she was going to agree to sell the house, sometimes even she thought she was going to agree to sell the house, but in the end they would be back where they started. Roy Bryce began to feel it would be better to see if he could buy some of their antiques. He knew Marjorie would be a tough negotiator, but he liked a challenge as much as she did. In fact he began to wonder whether they wouldn't make a good team. 'Play your cards right, my lad,' he told himself, 'and you may nab her *and* the furniture.'

When the flowers started to arrive, Molly was almost shocked. 'Sending you flowers at your age,' she said. Mrs Turtle on the other hand was rather gratified. 'Look at Joan Collins - flowers every day - in and out of bed with those handsome young men.'

'Yes, Mrs Turtle, and perhaps you'd clean the bath - ' Marjorie intervened.

'Indeed I will. No need to tell me,' and she made indignantly for the stairs.

Molly pondered. She didn't want to be unkind but however hard she tried she couldn't imagine Marjorie jumping in and out of bed with those glamorous television stars. They were pouncers and that was not Marjorie's line at all. Of course she didn't really know what her line was.

'You're quite pink, Molly. Are you feverish?' But Marjorie's mind was on other things. She started making a list, and Molly bustled off.

As the days went by Marjorie seemed to grow younger, and Roy Bryce's visits became ever more frequent. Molly began to be seriously worried. If Marjorie did marry Roy Bryce - but surely she wouldn't? She had been independent for too long. Yet it began to seem possible. Roy became proprietorial. He pecked Marjorie on the cheek and winked at Molly. It was terrible but there was an inevitability about it.

Marjorie finally broke the news to Molly, when they were alone together at breakfast. Molly put her tea cup down quite steadily.

'Are you sure it's wise Marjorie?'

'Wise Molly dear? Whatever do you mean? People do get married you know.'

'But you?'

'What is different about me?' She gave Molly a brisk half smile and checked the pins in her hair. 'Roy and I are very well suited. He doesn't want a lot of hanky panky.'

'Hanky panky?'

'Well, you know. Everything in its place. After all we're not young. But neither are we old. We'll make a social niche for ourselves.'

'A niche?'

'We've decided to move to Clacton-on-Sea.'

'Clacton-on-Sea?'

'Oh Molly, do stop repeating what I say. Yes, Roy's been asked to take over the Hacker and Hacker branch there. We'll go into the antiques business as well.'

Molly almost wailed. 'What will *I* do?'

'You'll stay on here and you'll take in a lodger. Two lodgers even. A married couple.'

'Oh Marjorie, you mean strangers?'

'They'll soon become friends,' Marjorie said, her tone daring them not to.

'But we never have friends - '

'Of course we do - well we did when we wanted them, and it's time we stirred ourselves.'

'It'll be alright for you,' Molly said. 'You'll have Mr - Roy.'

'And Roy knows all about letting. He can find you a really nice couple. Lots of people like to come to Bournemouth. It's the sea air.'

Molly felt that Marjorie was not giving the problem her usual attention. Imagine strangers living in the house. 'Oh Marjorie, would they sit and watch television with me? I wouldn't like that.' She imagined an old couple, snuffling and fidgeting, muttering together, changing the programme from *Coronation Street* to some quiz show, with alarming families competing for washing machines, and kissing each other and their opponents and the presenter or whatever he was - kissing his smiling, sweating face, kissing the bikini-clad girls who pulled the curtains back to show them their prizes - shrieking that they were 'over the moon' with delight. It was a nightmare.

Marjorie looked up from the list she was making and suddenly realised that Molly was about to cry.

'Now then Molly. Chin up. We won't leave you until it's all settled. Now we'll have to divide the furniture - I'm just making a list of it all. You'll keep your favourite things but after all, there's far too much about. And the room you let can have cheap things in it. In case they're clumsy or careless.'

This was Marjorie all right. No hesitation once she had decided. Molly had that old familiar feeling that everything would be all right if she left it to Marjorie. She wouldn't think about the lodgers, of how she could possibly cope without Marjorie's direction. It was best not to think about the future at all.

When the cheque came from the auctioneers even Marjorie was speechless. It was her habit to put the post beside her plate - somehow letters were nearly always addressed to her - take a piece of toast and very carefully spread it with butter and marmalade. She would pour out her coffee, take a bite of toast, flick a crumb or two off the front of her cardigan, and finally pick up an envelope and study it. Buff envelopes - and they nearly always were buff envelopes - had endlessly proved themselves to contain shocks of one kind or another. Yet Molly still had hopes of a happy conclusion. She would gaze at Marjorie as if at a conjurer whilst Marjorie studied the postmark, the mode of address, and commented on the various inaccuracies perpetrated by computers. This morning she was surprised. The envelope was a recycled off-white, quite thick, every detail on the front was correct and it bore a first-class stamp. On the back was embossed the name of an auctioneer.

'Ah, the stamps, Molly. I wonder if they sold them.'

She slit the envelope open with the extra knife Molly always laid out for that purpose, and took out a thick piece of paper to which was attached a cheque. Her mouth opened, but no words came. This was so extraordinary that for a moment Molly froze in her chair. Then as Marjorie shook out the letter and blinked Molly was reassured that she was not about to have a seizure. It must be good news.

'Is it a lot of money, Marjorie?' she asked anxiously.

Marjorie snapped her mouth shut and swallowed. She composed herself, took a sip of coffee and said in a slightly shaky voice: 'Two hundred thousand pounds!'

'It can't be. Marjorie it must be the computer. You always say they make mistakes. It must mean two hundred pounds - after all, they were *old* stamps - '

'That's the whole point, Molly. Apparently they were old and rare. You don't imagine new ones would fetch any money? But this - it's on the cheque in figures and writing, and it's in the letter. That's one hundred thousand pounds each!'

It was incredible. In unusual harmony they beamed at one another. Marjorie was thinking 'We could buy an antique shop' and Molly was thinking 'I needn't have lodgers.'

They finished their breakfasts, amidst murmurs of 'Who would have thought - ' and 'Dear Father, he was so clever - ' and 'Do you think he had any idea?' and 'Of course he did.' Until Marjorie suddenly became businesslike.

'We'll go straight to the bank and open two high interest deposit accounts, until we decide what to do with it. Come along Molly, Mrs Turtle can wash up.'

Mr Whalley called to his wife, 'The royal family's in a hurry today. They're almost trotting.'

'Perhaps they're on a health kick and think they're jogging,' said Mrs Whalley, with a pitying smile.

The sisters collected the paper from the Indian newsagent and even Marjorie replied to his greeting, Parsley and all.

After depositing the money in the bank they went to Claytons. Strange how good news makes things look so much better, thought Marjorie. Usually she was abrupt and pointed out coffee stains on the table cloth. Small children seemed to be noisy or to bump against her chair. But this morning she surprised the waitress with a smile, covered up the coffee stains with sugar bowl and ash tray, and made conciliatory sounds when a child blew a tin whistle close to her left ear. Naturally the waitress reported behind the scenes that the one what was usually so severe was all right really, probably has to look after the other one what smiles all the time.

After this there was no holding Roy. He was determined not to lose his opportunity of freedom, little realising that teaming up with Marjorie was the one way of ensuring he had no freedom at all. His flat in Bournemouth sold well, and he suggested that Marjorie should sell her half of Balmoral to Molly for £50,000. Marjorie explained to Molly that it would mean she could sell the house whenever she wanted.

All this responsibility thrown so suddenly on her shoulders left Molly paralysed with anxiety. How could Marjorie desert her after all these years? There was hardly a moment in her life when Molly had not felt secure in the knowledge that, whatever confronted her, Marjorie would be there to advise and direct.

Whilst furniture was packed and rooms left strangely bare, Molly tried to be helpful. Like an automaton she reacted to Marjorie's instructions. She and Mrs Turtle, who came in extra mornings to help, carried, cleaned and polished, and finally helped Marjorie to pack her own belongings. All the suitcases in the attic were old and heavy, so a new matching set was bought. Every now and then a pink-faced puffing Molly would murmur to Mrs Turtle 'How will I *manage*? What shall I *do*?' And Mrs Turtle, thoroughly enjoying the upheaval told her not to worry, she would be around to help. 'With what?' moaned Molly. 'There will only be me, alone in the house. Oh dear - '

'You'll sell it. Mr Bryce will see to it for you. He can arrange it through the office here.'

'Then what would I do?' Molly was aware that it was strange she should be asking Mrs Turtle, but then everything was strange. Marjorie seemed in another world and had quite thrown off her rôle model image.

She seemed almost to see Molly as a second Mrs Turtle. It was no good trying to get help from Marjorie, she just said idiotic things like 'The world's your oyster, Molly.' Molly was afraid of the world and didn't like oysters, and scuttled away to get on with the washing-up.

Breakfast had lost its pleasure. That moment when the sisters had sat together companionably, Marjorie opening the odd buff envelope and Molly round-eyed on being told of its contents, had completely gone. Marjorie scarcely sat down. She nibbled half a piece of toast and left her coffee to get cold. Buff envelopes there were, but they were opened hastily in the hall. There was no time to discuss their contents. It seemed to Molly that everything had changed the moment the cheque for the stamps arrived.

Suddenly arrangements for the wedding and departure went into top gear and she wondered whether perhaps Roy was really calling the tune. Whilst always deferring to Marjorie he had a way of suggesting something to her and then, whilst Marjorie was digesting it, he would say 'You're so wise, Marjorie. That's just what we should do', as if the idea had come from her. And Marjorie would look pleased and say something authoritative like 'Yes, I'm sure that's right. Will you see to the details?'

These thoughts would pop unexpectedly into Molly's mind, where they would be given short shrift. If Marjorie believed Roy Bryce was a good man then he was a good man. And anyway, what could be wrong with 'managing' Marjorie, except that it had never been done before.

They were married in the local Register Office on a windy day at the end of March, Roy looking very smart in a new blue pin-striped suit, with a Paisley tie, and Marjorie in a green suit with a white frilly blouse and a hat composed of a variety of different coloured flower petals. Molly and Mrs Turtle felt, as they looked, quite dowdy beside this almost yuppie couple. Throughout the short service the official looked very severe, as if he thought it was all a mistake. But in fact he had long ago lost his curiosity over the assorted couples over whom he had such strange power. Once he had felt conscious of bestowing happiness, of being part of a special occasion, but no longer. Too many of his joinings together had been put asunder. It had become a job like any other.

The ring was taken from the sinister square of black velvet on which it had lain and placed on Marjorie's finger. Molly thought of their parents and shed a tear or two, unable to make up her mind whether they would approve or not. Mrs Turtle patted her arm.

Signatures were briskly demanded and given, like ransoms, and it was all over. On the way out they passed the next wedding party and Marjorie sniffed. The couple were canoodling in a corner whilst far too many people, of assorted ages and states of inebriation, leaned against the walls. Two girls appeared to be dressed as bridesmaids and wore shiny pink dresses with short puffed sleeves. Their plump arms were blue with cold and their teeth chattered.

In the street Marjorie said 'How undignified,' and her retinue made various sounds of agreement. Roy had arranged a car and they all drove back to Balmoral.

Mrs Whalley called to her husband 'I think HRH has married that weedy chap from Hackers.'

Mr Whalley joined her at the window. 'Are you sure? A bit of a come down surely?'

'Last chance.'

'She's always smart.'

'Smart and bossy. That won't last.'

Three

Molly felt she would never get used to being alone. She was completely unable to make up her mind what to do. Should she leave Bournemouth? Go on a cruise? Take a course? Go into a convent? All the support she got from Marjorie was a picture postcard with the message 'Clacton very bracing. You must visit us when we are settled. Don't forget to pay TV licence end of April. Roy doing quite well.'

Mrs Turtle was full of suggestions at first but soon became bored. Molly was always so polite and unassuming. She never asked for anything to be done and always thanked Mrs Turtle for everything she did. It took the heart out of the job somehow. With Marjorie she knew her work was scrutinised in every detail so she did it well and was proud of the shine she got on the tallboy, or cleaning the brass handles on the desk without leaving a mark on the wood, and all the other tiresome jobs which Marjorie would set her to do. On the rare occasions when Marjorie did criticise, Mrs Turtle enjoyed being indignant and denying her fault whilst admiring Marjorie for spotting it. There was no challenge with Molly. She wouldn't mind if I sat in the kitchen and drank tea all morning, she thought.

'Now dear,' she said one morning when her work was done and she had eaten her cheese sandwich - she had taken to calling Molly dear, as if she were a child. 'I'm afraid I won't be able to do for you in the future. It's a long walk up from the centre and I'm not getting any younger.'

'Oh, Mrs Turtle!'

'Well, it's not as if you had anything to do. It's a pity you never trained for anything, but there you are.'

'I suppose I could train for something. I would have liked to be a nurse.'

'At your age? Never. There comes a time when it's too late to teach an old dog new tricks, as they say,' and Mrs Turtle chuckled, whilst folding up her overall for the last time, and putting out clean tea towels.

'Do they?' asked Molly. Who could have said it and why? When she was a child their next door neighbour had an old dog and they were always teaching it new tricks. Well, not tricks exactly, but to do useful things it hadn't done before. Anyway, nursing wasn't a trick and she wasn't a dog. Perhaps it was just as well that Mrs Turtle was leaving. She had changed. Without Marjorie nothing could be the same and she might as well get used to it. 'All right Mrs Turtle.'

'I'll get a job in one of those flats on the front. Modern block with a lift. After all, I must take care of my legs at my age - ' she seemed not to realise she had no battle on her hands.

'Yes Mrs Turtle, that would be nice,' and Molly opened her handbag. Taking out some notes she handed them to Mrs Turtle. 'This is what I owe you I think.'

Mrs Turtle thus stopped in her tracks was disappointed. She had expected shock, entreaties, tears even, and she had been ready for an invigorating half hour of explanations, followed by reminiscences of old times, perhaps being told what a tower of strength she had been to them all. She had even been going to say 'If you ever need me you know where to find me.' So it was with a feeling of anti-climax that she put on her coat and knotted her scarf under her chin.

'Well I'll be off then,' she said.

Molly opened the back door. 'Good-bye Mrs Turtle. I expect I'll see you in town.'

'No doubt you will dear,' and with casual good-byes their years of closeness and apparent understanding dissipated on the cool April air.

Like a book, thought Molly. Another chapter in her life finished. But what had she done with her life? All the chapters belonged to others, never to her. She looked at her face in the glass above the marble mantelpiece. She saw a plump, pleasant woman with blue eyes gazing back at her. Hair rather a mess - she hadn't had it done since Marjorie left. It was 'pepper and salt' as they say, she thought. She wished she were one of 'them' to say these things. But she had no-one to say them to now even if she wanted to. She thought of the house when the four of them first moved in. It had somehow never occurred to any of them that they would not be there, together, for ever. She supposed everyone lived like that. If you thought about death when there was so much in the present to be thankful for you would be thought morbid, and probably end up in the psychiatrist's chair.

'Pull yourself together Molly,' Marjorie would have said. Father would have advised a stiff upper lip. What would Mother have said? 'Go and have your hair done and buy a pair of shoes. If your head and your feet are all right you can tackle anything.' Molly wasn't quite sure of the last bit, but she thought that must be her mother's reasoning. She remembered her giving that advice to some vague, grey relative who had actually visited them in the dim distant past, recovering from a bereavement.

'I *will*,' said Molly out loud. And the face in the glass said 'I *will*,' and smiled rather anxiously.

Once she had done both these things she did feel better. Her feet were comfortable and her reflection in shop windows was almost smart. She walked along the front and for the first time since Marjorie left she went into Claytons. She had bought the Daily Telegraph on her way down. 'How is other Parsley?' the Indian asked her kindly. 'Very well thank you - but she's Mrs Bryce now.' 'Not so nice as Parsley,' he said, and beamed on Molly.

It was strange to be in Claytons on her own, but not as bad as she had expected it would be. She ordered coffee and settled down to do the quick crossword. It was full of vague clues like 'A girl's name', 'A tree', 'A garden implement' and her mind wandered. A girl's name - Molly. A tree - that oak tree in the garden she used to lie under on long summer days. A garden implement - old Mr Hooker, hoeing the herbaceous border. Mr Hooker had been the kind of person who could never finish a conversation, and so she used to try not to start one. But he had such a good, serious face, and was so serene she could not help it, and when it was time to go in to lunch they were left there saying to each other 'That's it then,' and 'Right you are then - the marigolds will be up soon - ' 'Will they?' 'Yes me dear, then the sweet peas - ' 'The sweet peas, how lovely.' 'Yes, and then - '

Thinking of Mr Hooker, Molly was surprised when there was a commotion at the entrance to Claytons and the man causing it turned out not to be Mr Hooker. She would not have been at all surprised to see his kindly face, and she was already half smiling in greeting. But what she saw was a man who looked exactly like a character in an amateur dramatic performance described as 'peppery retired Colonel'. He was grey haired, what was left of it, and had a moustache. He was stockily built, pink-faced, with watery blue eyes, and he wore a monocle. 'Bloody door' he barked, pushing it over a small pebble on which it had stuck for a moment.

There were one or two ladies on their own and Molly was absurdly pleased that he chose her table. Not that she liked the look of him very much, but it was as if they were all on show and he had made a deliberate choice. 'Mind if I sit here m'dear?' he asked, sitting down heavily.

'No - no. I mean please do.' Molly was a little flustered. She felt she should ignore him but somehow she couldn't. He made such a fuss. He shifted his chair, dropped his walking stick, grunted as he retrieved it, knocked Molly's knee, and apologised - it seemed as if he would never get settled and Molly was bound to react, even looking guilty, as if she were the cause of it all. Eventually he sat back in his chair. 'Like doll's house chairs, what?' and he glared at Molly.

'I'm afraid they are,' she said apologetically.

'Not your fault.'

'No.'

'You drinking chocolate?'

'No, I'm afraid I'm drinking coffee.'

'Nothing to be afraid of. They say it's bad for you. Don't believe 'em.' He raised his voice. 'Miss - a cup of coffee please. And another for my friend here.'

And that was that. They were apparently friends. 'Jessop,' he said. 'Archibald Jessop. Colonel - retired.'

That was enough for Molly. She had a strange idea that all Army officers came out of the same mould as her father, and she had trusted her father implicitly.

She and Archibald Jessop took to meeting at Claytons for coffee every morning, then walking along the front. Sometimes they sat in a shelter, looking out to sea. Their conversation was never very animated. The Colonel barked out a few comments on the weather, and sometimes on the boarding house in which he lived. It appeared to be expensive, dirty, uncomfortable and full of very tiresome people.

When Molly told him about Balmoral he perked up. 'House of your own, eh? Lucky girl.'

Molly blushed at being called a girl. She knew she wasn't a girl any more yet it made her feel good. To her dismay she heard herself saying 'I could let you a room. I mean, that was what my sister said I should do. Let a room, I mean.'

'My dear girl. How very kind. You're a dear, sweet girl - ' and he sprang to his feet more swiftly than he had ever done before. He waved his stick at the sea, shouted 'Yo ho!' and turned to the anxious figure of Molly, now looking rather apprehensive. Giving her no time to change her mind he shouted 'Come along, my dear. Take me to Balmoral,' and he held out his hand.

Archibald Jessop had really fallen on his feet. When he first left the Army he had thought it a simple matter to find a wife. He had understood that Bournemouth was full of unattached ladies of a certain age. It wasn't as if he wanted a dolly bird. Lots of men of his age - he was fifty-nine - wouldn't look at a woman over forty. But he wasn't fussy. He'd had a go at sex when he was stationed in the Far East. Had an affair that went quite well for a while. But really she had made all the running. He was always being bundled into bed when he would rather be drinking, and woken up in the night by fond caresses when he would far rather be asleep. Not that he hadn't managed to perform when called upon. But he had never really loved anyone. 'Can't all be great lovers, what?' he used to say with refreshing candour when conquests were being boasted of in the Mess. He had no really close friends, male or female. In his younger days he had drinking companions, and he laughed a lot. But in fact he had no sense of humour, no warmth, no imagination. As the years went by he became irritable. Money was short. And the wealthy widows never turned up.

Molly was a godsend. And to her he seemed a godsend. His fierce appearance and humourless, dogmatic approach to things seemed to fill the gap left in her life by her sister's departure. He also needed looking after, and this was something Molly knew all about.

Archibald Jessop had never lived so well. Molly asked very little for his bed and board and fed him magnificently. After he started going to the pub in the evening - Molly refused to go with him, her father had said pubs were no places for ladies - she felt lonely. 'Shall I get in some sherry?' she asked one day, 'then you could have a drink here in the evenings.'

'Capital idea, but make it whisky, my dear,' said the Colonel.

Little by little the whisky order increased from a bottle a fortnight to a bottle a week, and then two, but Molly didn't mind. They sat on the sofa watching television and she was content. Archibald tended to doze off but that was no problem. Whenever there was an explosion of temper or laughter on the screen he opened bleary eyes, smiled vaguely at Molly as if not quite sure where he was, took another gulp of his whisky and dropped off again.

Some evenings he stayed awake longer than others, and on one of these occasions Molly asked him about his family. 'Had a brother once,' he said. 'Well, still have I suppose. Years younger than me. God knows where he is. Meant to keep mother and father together after the war. Didn't of course. Even I could see that wouldn't work. Got married. Left his wife. Lived in Clapham.' He paused. 'Had a daughter. Must be six or thereabouts.'

Molly was excited. 'Perhaps his wife and child *still* live there. Have you got the address?'

'Daresay. Somewhere. Hardly know them.'

'You could ask them down for the day.'

'Why?'

'It's nice to have a family.'

'Your sister never comes.'

'Well, they're starting a business - they're very busy. Marjorie often sends a postcard. I wrote to tell her I had a lodger - '

'Hah!'

Molly jumped. 'I mean a paying guest.'

'Never trust lodgers. Come and go.' Then abruptly, 'Call me Archie.'

Molly had somehow never called him anything so it wouldn't be difficult.

'Archie is much nicer that Archibald,' she said thoughtfully. 'Less prickly.'

'Like me, eh?'

'Yes,' she said, not sure whether he was prickly or less prickly. She felt in all honesty he was prickly, or else why did she have to say things in the way he wanted to hear them? Perhaps she misjudged him because she wasn't accustomed to his barking delivery. And when he frowned and his eyebrows shot up to meet each other above his nose she felt almost frightened. But it was a pleasurable fright and somehow gave her a sense of security. Imagine the effect he would have on a burglar. Anyway she was accustomed to someone else being in charge and had missed it in those first few weeks after Marjorie left. When Archie started calling her Molly it seemed right and natural.

Molly took the soap operas they watched very seriously. 'Oh dear, he's going to leave her and go off with that girl. It's too bad. After all she's done for him.'

Archie took a swig of whisky and snorted. 'Only a yarn!'

'They seem real to me. I feel as if I know them. Oh look, she's really upset.'

'What happened to that chap who stole the lease? Liked him. Got his head screwed on.'

'But he's dead! Surely you remember? He fell under a tram.'

'Tram? Where'd he find a tram? Clever chap. Not many trams around. Trust him. Buses are two a penny.'

Molly gave a confused laugh. She often wondered what he meant but she was getting used to him, as if he had always been around. When they went out together Molly took quick, short steps, appearing almost to run to keep up with him.

Archie told the man in the newspaper shop not to call Molly 'Parsley' but 'Madam' and now he called her 'Madam Parsley', which Molly found rather embarrassing. It made her think of Madam Butterfly.

The Whalleys next door were not quite sure what to make of this new turn of events. 'Seems to have found a man to take her sister's place. He walks ahead, just like the sister did, and she's still trotting along, looking amiable. Talk about dark horses.'

'Perhaps she advertised for him,' said Mrs Whalley.

'What - "Reliable man needed, to take the place of sister" - '

'It does seem strange.' Mrs Whalley laughed in a superior fashion.

'Next thing we know there'll be another wedding,' said Mr Whalley.

'Don't be absurd, not *that* one.' Mrs Whalley laughed again, and admired her own slim figure in the long mirror on their bedroom wall.

In *Coronation Street* things were moving. A middle-aged couple were getting married and everyone seemed pleased. Molly thought, she's about my age. She might even be older. Her neck looks rather older. But she is vivacious, that's true. She looked at Archie. His eyes bulged slightly as he swallowed his whisky and she thought, he's about *his* age. Archie turned to Molly, the almost neat whisky coursing through his veins. 'Molly my girl, how about it?'

'About what?' Molly gasped, somehow knowing what he meant.

'You and me, eh? Getting together?'

'You mean - ?'

'Marrying - how about it?'

'Oh Archie!' She was delighted. 'Oh yes, Archie. How lovely.'

'Jolly good,' he said, and grabbed her hand.

Molly was torn between the screen and the events in her own sitting room, unsure which was which. She took a deep breath and turned to Archibald Jessop. But he was asleep.

Four

After a lot of cajoling Archie produced the address of his sister-in-law in Clapham. Molly wrote and asked if she and her little girl could come to the wedding and to her astonished pleasure Emily Jessop replied that they would love to come. The only problem was money. Could Colonel Jessop pay their fares?

Colonel Jessop had cash to spare these days and the chance of more, so that was no problem. Molly had told him about the money from the stamp sale and he couldn't believe his luck. He had guessed she had savings and he knew he wouldn't have much difficulty in getting his hands on all that was going once they were married. But here was a lump sum right away, and he knew just how to make it more. One of the chaps he met at the pub, ex-Army, far from down-and-out, had just made a packet, so he said, out of a mine in West Africa. If Archie had had the ready cash he could have done the same. You only had to know the right people - and the far from down-and-out chap had tapped his nose and winked. Later, Archie had thought, once we're married, then we'll see. But now there was no need to wait.

'Molly, my girl, your money's rotting in the bank.'

'I get good interest,' said Molly proudly. 'It's in a special reserve account.'

'I'll double it for you - give me a month and I'll double it.'

'No, Archie, Father wouldn't agree.'

'You bet he would. No army man would miss a chance like this. I'll go down to the pub tonight. See if Bob's there. Bring him back and introduce you. Jolly good chap - seen service in the Far East. Trust him with the Crown Jewels.'

Bob Lucking accepted Archie's invitation with alacrity.

He and Archie sat on the sofa, each clutching a large tumbler, the whisky bottle on the table between them. Molly sat in the armchair, facing the television set. She had politely turned the sound down but couldn't help watching. As Bob expounded on the mining situation in West Africa the man on the screen was busy with his hand in the till, glancing surreptitiously over his shoulder.

'No problem,' said Bob. 'Make out a cheque to the Brassbound Consolidated Mining Fund and Bob's your uncle,' he laughed too loudly. 'Bob's your uncle, eh?' He had a plausible look, like the man on the screen. They both looked at Molly and away again. 'I don't trust you at all. I'm sure you're up to no good,' Molly said vehemently.

Bob Lucking started back in surprise. He had a soft round face, watery eyes of an indeterminate colour, and fading ginger hair. His mouth, previously working to his bidding, suddenly fell open and something gold from within flashed.

Archie jumped to his feet. 'What are you saying?' he barked. 'Molly, look at me.'

She took her eyes off the screen with difficulty and was surprised by the faces of the two men, so changed with hurt and anger.

'What d' you mean you don't trust him?'

'Well,' said Molly, taken aback, 'well, after all he may work in the shop but he shouldn't take money out of the till. Look at him - he's scooped out two handfuls of money and stuffed it in his pockets. You can't say that's right?' Molly was flushed and agitated.

Archie crossed over and snapped off the television set. Bob pulled himself together, gave a weak smile, and said 'Quite so, Ma'am, quite so.'

'Sorry old chap,' said Archie. 'Thought she meant - too much television - thinks they're real. Molly, you've upset Bob here.'

'Oh dear, I'm so sorry.' And she really was. She still was not quite sure why anyone was upset, and she would do anything to make it up to them, as Archie realised. 'Never mind,' he said, chuckling. 'It's just your way. No harm in it. Now listen to Bob - knows how to invest money - carry on old chap.'

By the end of the evening a beaming Molly had handed over the cheque, having been assured it was a silver mine, only called Brassbound because it was so safe.

'Imagine a strong chest with brass corners and a brass lock. Security, that's what it stands for,' explained Bob. 'Your money will be as safe as if it were in that box.'

'I *see*,' said Molly, pleased that everyone was happy again.

'See you at the wedding then,' said Bob as he left, his brown trilby hat at a jaunty angle, his thick teddy bear coat belted tightly against the night air.

'Good-oh,' shouted Archie. 'I'll let you know - '

Molly waved, smiling uncertainly. 'The wedding?'

'Our wedding, old girl.' It was the first time he had called her old girl and she didn't like it very much. His gallantry, such as it was, was beginning to wear off as he became totally confident of achieving all his goals.

The day before the wedding, arranged for 2.30 at the Register Office, Marjorie rang from Clacton. 'I'm afraid we can't be there, Molly. Roy's got a sale on and I have to stay in the office. We'll come and see you soon. Good luck,' she finished briskly.

Their father had ingrained in them the folly of wasting money on long distance calls. When they were young every three minutes a series of bleeps, like radio time signals, came over the wires, warning you of your extravagance. Even if they were in the middle of explaining why one or the other was in the school sanatorium when three minutes were up their father would shout 'The pips!' and smartly hang up on them. Molly remembered once he hung up just as Marjorie was saying that school was breaking up a day early because of chicken pox, and it caused no end of unpleasantness. They were left in the front hall, alone with the dreaded Miss Potts, who finally took them home herself, by train and taxi. Such a protracted period spent in the company of Miss Potts was a strain even on Marjorie, and they arrived home pale and exhausted. Their parents immediately concluded that they had perpetrated some awful deed and had been expelled, and as Miss Potts was too irritated to be helpful it was some time before the confusion was cleared up.

So Marjorie's present attitude towards long distance calls was not what upset Molly. What hurt her very deeply was what she felt to be a betrayal. She herself would have attended Marjorie's wedding however difficult it was to manage it. How could she go to that Register Office with only Archie and Bob Lucking? Of course there would be Emily and Alma, but she didn't know them. She needed someone there who knew her, and even who knew her parents.

Molly suddenly thought of Mrs Turtle. She would do. She had known their parents, she had been at

Marjorie's wedding, and she always knew what was what. Perhaps she would come along beforehand so as to make sure Molly had everything right.

Mrs Turtle was delighted to be invited to the wedding. She was also pleased that Molly needed her support and advice, and she even offered to meet her and help her to buy her wedding outfit. 'I really am surprised - imagine *you*.' And she was agog to meet this man who was prepared to take on the diffident Molly. Those Passley sisters were certainly deep. If anyone had suggested that after their parents died they would find themselves husbands she would have laughed in their faces. She could not imagine who might have said this to her - perhaps those inquisitive people who lived next door to Balmoral. She often saw them peering out of a window or over a hedge. They certainly missed nothing. But Mrs Turtle had long ago decided not to talk to either of them since they obviously thought far too much of themselves. Mrs Turtle had always enjoyed it when she passed them, holding her head very high and with her nose in the air.

Their shopping expedition went very well and they ended up at Claytons having a slap up tea of scones and cakes. The festive atmosphere brought them close and suddenly it was as if they had never parted company. Mrs Turtle was very interested in the Colonel's sister-in-law and niece. She thought they would be good company for Molly in the future. It was agreed that Mrs Turtle would come along in the morning on the day of the wedding and see to the food. A buffet lunch beforehand and a nice tea afterwards. She would make sure Molly looked her best and, most interesting of all, she would meet Colonel Jessop. Molly's description of him had not been very encouraging, and as Molly tended to see the best in everyone this was not a good sign. But Mrs Turtle's only requirement was that he would either be far nicer and more attractive than she expected, or an absolute disaster. She would almost prefer the latter since she would later on be called upon to advise, commiserate and produce gems from her store of aphorisms.

The wedding day arrived and with it Emily and Alma. Emily was thin and pale, with large brown eyes and dark wavy hair cut rather badly. She didn't make the best of herself, but perhaps that was the result of Archie's brother's betrayal.

'I'm sorry your sister couldn't come after all,' she said to Molly, 'You should have had a relation too.'

'May I be your relation?' asked Alma, who had been listening to their introductions. She looked a lot like her mother except that her face was rounder, her hair was lighter, and her eyes were blue. She had a fringe which almost covered her eyebrows. Molly was charmed. 'How very kind of you. It will be lovely to have you as my relative. What a pretty dress.'

Alma was happy in her old blue dress, rather short now. She knew it looked nice, it matched her eyes, and she had been disappointed when her mother had seemed upset that they could not buy her something new.

Molly looked well in the demure flowered two-piece which Mrs Turtle had advised as 'suitable' and a small close fitting hat of blue material, matching one of the flowers in her outfit.

There was a moment after lunch when Molly and Emily were alone upstairs and Emily said anxiously: 'I do hope Archie makes a good husband. Bernard is quite a bit younger than him. Perhaps he's more settled.'

'What happened, Emily? Why did Bernard leave you? I'm sorry, I shouldn't ask.'

'Oh I don't mind. It was perfect to begin with but after Alma arrived he seemed to lose interest in us. He couldn't share you see.' She sighed. 'Then he started to drink. He was always in the pub, lost money at the betting shop. One day I said "You should live in that pub" and he said "All right I will." And he packed his bag and left. I don't know where he really went. The only thing I've heard is that he wants to sell the house and we'll have to move out.'

Molly's sympathetic reply was drowned by a bellow from Archie in the hall - 'Come on you two, it's time to go,' and Alma rushed up to give them each a pink rose which she had picked in the garden.

'I've broken off the prickles,' she said.

And each clutching a rose they went down to Archie. He hadn't agreed to a taxi. 'Breath of sea air will do you good,' he'd said. So off they went down the road, to the intense interest of Mr Whalley who was weeding his front garden.

'Keep an eye open,' he said to his wife when he went indoors. 'They'll be back. Another wedding. You mark my words.'

'I don't believe it. Even she couldn't be taken in by that dreadful looking man. They're probably taking the girl to the pier. There's a play on - *Bluebell in Fairyland*.'

'It's little Miss Balmoral who's in fairyland, my dear. There must be some money there. He knows he's on to a good thing.'

'Don't be unkind,' said Mrs Whalley, patting her hair and moving to the mirror over the fireplace. Poor soul, she thought, if she's really married him. Well, I suppose it's better than nothing and after all she's no beauty she thought, giving herself a knowing look.

Bob Lucking was waiting outside the Register Office, and if Molly hadn't been feeling so happy she would have been taken aback. But she just thought how nice that he looked so cheerful in his check plus fours, with his green hacking jacket over a yellow pullover. His brown and white check shirt didn't look too bad - perhaps the red bow tie was a mistake. But Molly smiled at him and he greeted her effusively. 'Charming, Ma'am. Charming. You remind me of my sister. She married a sailor. I'm not sure where they are now, but I'm sure they're happy.'

He turned to Archie. 'All set?' he asked.

'Yes, yes. In we go,' said Archie testily.

The ceremony was over in a flash and Molly felt quite blasé, knowing the ropes as she did. She told them all, even Mrs Turtle, where to stand and was prepared for the official's very plain English. No 'thee' or 'thou' which would have made it sound much more mystical, but at least there could be no mistake about 'Will you take him for your husband?' and 'That's it then,' after Archie had agreed to take her for his wife. The square of black velvet lay on the desk as before, but the ring seemed to spend less time on it than at Marjorie's wedding. Short cuts probably meant another wedding could be slotted in. Very wise, Molly thought.

Once in the street, Molly asked Bob Lucking if he would like to come back to tea and he was delighted. Mrs Turtle gave one of her sniffs. She had sized up

Bob Lucking and found him wanting. They all piled into a taxi which had just deposited another couple outside the Register Office. Bob Lucking squeezed up against Emily, much to her disgust - he smelled of a man who seldom bathed and never washed his clothes properly. She thought of a report she'd read in a newspaper recently of a man who hadn't changed his clothes for twenty-seven years.

'Uncle Archie, I'm glad you married Aunt Molly. I'm going to like her.'

'Jolly good. All get on well together. That's the ticket.'

Tea was laid out and Mrs Turtle, who had been taking rather a back seat during the ceremony, came into her own. She brought in the large silver tea pot which hadn't been used since both parents were alive. Everyone ate heartily, as if they had been for a walk rather than to a quick wedding. No-one, however, ate more than Bob Lucking. Alma watched him eat the last cup cake. 'You're very hungry, aren't you?' she said. 'Are you poor?'

'Poor?' Bob Lucking looked at her in astonishment. She had exactly assessed his position. No-one before had ever challenged his assertion that he had money in the bank, mining shares paying large dividends and lump sums on the way, and he couldn't think how to explain this to a child, especially one giving him such a direct and honest look. Crumbs fell on his chin as he said again, with a contrived laugh, 'Poor? Not me. What a funny girl you are. Your Uncle Archie will tell you - he knows me,' and, with another false laugh, he grabbed his cup and took a gulp of tea.

'Now Alma this won't do,' said Archie. 'Not at all. He isn't poor. What d'you mean by asking that?'

Alma was shame-faced and Emily held her protectively. Mrs Turtle, however, gave her an admiring look. Very perceptive she thought her.

'She's been hearing about poor people in Ethiopia at school,' said Emily. 'She thinks anyone who's hungry must be starving. I'm sorry Mr Lucking, but you did seem hungry.'

'Hungry? Not me. Going out to dinner tonight. In fact I'd better be off. Got to have a bath and a change.' And as he got to his feet the ladies looked at him in some disbelief. All four statements were suspect, but Molly jumped to her feet and said kindly, 'Bob, it was so good of you to come. We're going to the Isle of Wight for a few days - '

'Oh, a honeymoon!' said Alma, delighted.

'Well - I suppose so.' Molly looked doubtful. Then, turning back to Bob, 'You must come and see us when we get back.'

'That's right,' said Archie. 'Lunch or something, what?'

'Yes, indeed. Well, thank you for my tea. I hope to see you again Ma'am,' he said to Emily, flashing her a gold crowned smile, to which Emily replied, with a marked lack of enthusiasm, 'Good-bye, Mr Lucking,' and Archie led him away.

'Well' said Emily, 'where did Archie find him? I'm sure he was never a friend of yours.'

'No, well, we had very few friends. Archie met him at the pub - when he used to go there - he doesn't now of course.'

'Of course not. I do hope you'll be happy Molly. We must keep in touch.'

'We will,' promised Molly. She gazed at her new found family and sighed contentedly. This was her life starting - her chapter at last.

On the journey home to Clapham, Emily thought about Molly. She was delightful. She was naive certainly, but warm and caring. It was strange how good sometimes came out of bad. She doubted very much whether Archibald Jessop was going to be a good husband. Molly was too gentle, she would never be able to deal with him. He was the sort of man who would be a bully given half a chance, and he was likely to have every chance. Meanwhile Emily was delighted to have a new relation. There was nothing she needed more.

Emily and Bernard had been very much in love when they married. He had left his college job and worked from home for some insurance company. He had managed to get a loan from the bank and bought a computer, a fax machine, a telephone answering machine and a small gadget to keep in his pocket, which would call him up occasionally with a message. It was embarrassing if this happened when they were out, but they were both in that state of euphoria where such happenings could only end in laughter and bring them closer together.

At first all his machines chattered together happily, but after a while the fact that he was seldom there to listen to them seemed to lessen their enthusiasm, and after two years of blissful incompetence Bernard found himself without work. The machines sat silent in his 'study', the insurance firm dispensed with his services and he was forced to look for another job.

To Emily's surprise he soon fixed himself up as office manager to a large firm of building contractors in Clapham, near where they lived. This was fortunate as Emily was expecting a baby. She was sad that Bernard didn't seem very pleased about it. They had always said they didn't need children - they were enough for each other, but when Emily ran out of pills one weekend she thought it wouldn't matter one way or the other. When she was sure about the baby, she found she was delighted. Looking back she could see that the change in Bernard started around this time. Their long honeymoon was over.

The Christmas before Alma was born there was an office party, a form of entertainment which Emily particularly hated. Her pregnancy didn't show so she found herself being chatted up by various unpleasant office Lotharios, in particular one Ted Brackett. Whilst Ted leered at Emily, Bernard was busy making up to the Managing Director's secretary. Once home, Bernard said he had no interest in the girl it was just a way of keeping in with the Managing Director, which didn't seem very logical. He had not seemed to notice Ted's attentions to Emily.

On leaving a New Year's Eve party given by one of Bernard's colleagues in Kensington, Emily went up to the bedroom to fetch her coat. There she was pounced on by a man who said he was a gatecrasher. He seemed very proud of the fact. In the light from the landing she could see he was tall, and when he stood between her and the door, his silhouette was large and menacing. Fortunately someone else came dashing upstairs, snapped on the light, and started searching for a coat on the bed. The man slipped out of the door and Emily found her coat. At the door she paused, looking back at the bed and the strange array of coats on which she would have been ravished. Although the man had started to push her backwards, and she had been aware of his strength which would easily have overpowered her, all she could think was how much better the coat-covered bed than the hard floor. She wondered why she had made no sound. Bernard's new off-hand attitude towards her hurt her deeply and she seemed to be living in a dream. Perhaps she had felt that if she were raped Bernard would be bound to go mad with rage and jealousy. Or would he? At any rate she would tell him that it was a near thing, and surely he would feel something.

At the bottom of the stairs she found Bernard waiting impatiently.

'Come on. What have you been doing?'

'I was nearly raped as a matter of fact.'

'Yes, well. It's late and I've got to be in the office on time this morning. Good God, I've got to be there in four hours!'

Emily just had time to say to their hostess, 'There was a man in your bedroom who said he was a gatecrasher,' and to hear her reply 'Cheek!' as Bernard bundled her down the path.

After Alma was born Bernard started to drink heavily. In fact he developed what Emily recognised to be a 'drink problem'. Half empty bottles would turn up all over the house and if Emily pointed them out he would say 'Half empty? Half full I call it,' and take a swig from the bottle in question. It was not surprising that he drifted off. He simply could not take the responsibility of having a family. And as soon as Emily became a mother, to him she was only a mother. He saw them as mother and child, as it might be Virgin and Child, and this was not his scene.

When Emily pointed out how good Alma was he said 'Then why do you spend so much time with her?'

'I can hardly leave her alone.'

'Well I can't be doing with her around all the time.'

'So what am I supposed to do with her?'

'That's your problem.'

That was more or less the last conversation they had together.

After he had left, Emily did ring the office a couple of times but they said he hadn't been in for two weeks, and if he didn't show up by the end of the month his services would be dispensed with. It was Ted who told her this.

'You on your tod then?' he asked.

'Oh no, my parents have moved in,' said Emily quickly. A grunted 'Oh' greeted this lie, and Ted hung up.

Conjuring up her parents to put Ted off seemed suddenly to have brought them to life. For a while she was convinced she and Alma were not alone in the house and any moment she would find a woman in the kitchen, or a couple in the living room. It was eerie and she determined never to tell a serious lie again. You could live a lie if you weren't careful. When people assumed she had a husband at home she could pretend she had. She could make up stories about what they did together, of what fun they had. She remembered when, as a child, she had gone with other children from Barnardo's to do jobs in the village there had been a lady who used to call out to her mother in the back room. She'd say 'Don't be surprised to hear children's voices. They've come over from Barnardo's.' Or, 'I'll come and read to you when they've gone.' They were never allowed to go in her mother's room and they used to imagine that she was grotesque and mustn't be seen. She had grown a long nose out of all proportion to her face - she was cross-eyed and had a hare lip. All kinds of things. She never answered her daughter. Perhaps she was dumb. In the end when the lady died it turned out that there was no-one in the back room.

That should have been a lesson to me, thought Emily.

In fact Emily had never known her parents and had been brought up in a Barnardo's Home. She had been a lovely child and her photograph once appeared on the front cover of the Barnardo magazine, *The Ever Open Door*. Thousands of people must have been moved by the sight of those large, rather mournful brown eyes, the dark curly hair and the trusting smile, and although there had been many requests to adopt her none had worked out. Perhaps Barnardo's were reluctant to let her go. She became a little mother as she grew older, and had a calming and sweet influence on the other children, especially those coming in who were often in a state of shock bordering on autism. When it was time for thought to be given to her moving into the outside world the Home had offered her a job, and she had easily slipped into the adult rôle of house mother whilst being given time to attend a local college to study shorthand and typing. It was on this diploma course that she met Bernard, who was teaching in the computer department.

No-one had laid siege to Emily before and she was swept off her feet. Her friends at Barnardo's were delighted when they got engaged and helped with all the wedding arrangements. It was a modest affair but with so many willing helpers it was possible to have what seemed to Emily a fairy tale wedding. The older children and staff helped her make her wedding dress, and the cook made a splendid wedding cake. There were flowers everywhere in the Home, and in the local church. Although Bernard was told to ask anyone he liked to the wedding and the reception he only invited two friends from the college. He had an elder brother who he said was a pain and would ruin any celebration, and he had lost touch with his parents years ago. Emily had seen so many children cast aside, 'given away', that she was not surprised. She even felt this brought them closer together - they were both waifs, and would look after each other.

Wherever Bernard was now it seemed that he was still paying the mortgage on their house since no mortgage company had contacted her. Emily had applied for social security and was able to pay her way, and Alma was allocated to a nursery school. She took a part-time job and was able to take Alma to school in the morning and collect her at lunch time.

Emily was intrigued by the nursery school. It had the reputation of being one of the best in the area but the Headmistress was always absent, giving lectures on how to run the best nursery school. Meanwhile there were two uneducated nursery nurses, to comfort any child who cried, to put plasters on to grazes and imagined injuries, and to wash towels and tea cloths. There was a part-time black trainee and a supercilious girl doing her final practical stint before becoming a fully-trained nursery teacher. She appeared not to like adults, let alone children, and Emily wondered what on earth had brought her into the profession.

Teaching was frowned upon. Children must do as they pleased, opening up like flowers in this perfect ambience. Since there were twenty children in the morning, another twenty in the afternoon, and a further twenty who were there all day it was not possible for the small number of untrained staff to do more than run behind them picking up what they had dropped, and supervise them in the L-shaped playground.

Emily had seen the black trainee go to the 'modelling table' one day and start to take small pieces of plasticine from the large, unappealing ball thereon, and make small figures. In a moment she was surrounded by eager little faces, and soon they all started to make models, chattering and telling each other what they were doing. But this happy scene was broken up by the supercilious student teacher, saying something to the effect that 'the children must be left to make their own discoveries. When they take some plasticine from the whole, and return it, they are abstracting the theory of the conservation of volume.' The trainee looked blank and uncomprehending. The plasticine was replaced. The children dispersed.

At the end of the morning Emily was handed some daubs which Alma had done with powdered paints, mostly hand prints which seemed to be considered particularly creative, and had been hung on a string with others, all carefully labelled. Most parents threw them in the bin by the door, but Emily felt this rather cruel and would take them home and dispose of them when Alma wasn't looking.

When Alma moved on to Primary School, Emily was able to work longer hours but her interest in typing house particulars had waned. At first she laid these out with great precision, and liked making little boxes at the sides for 'VIEW BY APPOINTMENT' or 'KEYS WITH AGENT', but now she needed a break. She felt that taking Alma to school, going to work, collecting Alma and going home to supper and bed was her whole future. The invitation to Archibald's wedding was just what she needed to take her out of herself. Bernard had said Archibald was 'an old bore', and no doubt he would be marrying someone equally boring, but she went to Bournemouth determined to find something to enjoy. Archibald *was* an old bore, but Molly was pure gold.

Five

The Isle of Wight was not a great success. Archie and Molly stayed in a small hotel in Yarmouth, overlooking the harbour. It could have been the perfect spot but Archie was a total let-down. Molly hadn't expected much of him but every night he insisted on staying in the bar until it was empty, Molly sitting at a small unsteady table, fiddling with a glass of sherry, whilst Archie was up and down, having another whisky, chatting to people at the bar. When they finally got to the bedroom Archie used the bathroom first. Molly followed, and when she was ready for bed Archie was sound asleep and snoring.

Molly thought it strange that Archie was perfectly happy to watch sex and married bliss on television yet didn't seem to think they had anything to do with *his* married life. But of course she didn't know what he thought. And being accustomed to behave as others wished her to behave Molly pushed all such thoughts - even slight yearnings - into the back of her mind. After all she was better off than she was after Marjorie left. She had company and she had someone to look after.

It would have been nice to have been able to discuss things with Marjorie. But discuss what? Discuss sex with Marjorie? Unthinkable. But perhaps the matter could come casually into the conversation.

'Is Roy - very amorous?' No, that would certainly not do.

'Does Roy like to go to bed early?' or 'Is he a light sleeper?'

None of this was very good. It was all right to think about talking companionably with Marjorie but face to face was another matter. She would probably bark 'Roy?' as if you had used the wrong name, and if that didn't sink you she would raise her eyebrows and say 'amorous?' as if it was a pornographic word. Despite being philosophical she was disappointed. Married life was obviously not always like the novels she had read - or television for that matter. Again she thought of Joan Collins, whisked off her feet by admirers and carried off to bed to be almost eaten alive - Molly looked mistily out to sea. Archie's voice brought her back to reality.

'What are you thinking about, old girl. Your lost youth? Hah!'

She jumped and blushed. If only she were.

Their return to Balmoral caused no great stir. Only the Whalleys were at all interested, and now that all the unexpected happenings were over even they were losing interest.

At the Indian newspaper shop Molly said shyly 'I'm Mrs Jessop now.' 'That is good Parsley. I wish you all happiness. Sister is pleased?' 'Oh yes,' said Molly, though she was surprised to have heard no more from Marjorie since the day before their wedding.

Life moved along quietly and for a while Archie enjoyed his comfort, his food and drink, his devoted slave. He had been disgruntled to find that without her savings Molly had only a moderate income, just enough to keep him in the style to which he had become accustomed. He started to slope off to the pub again to 'see old Bob'.

'Bring him back here, Archie,' Molly kept saying, but in fact he would only be a distraction and she was now involved with several soaps on television and she hated missing any of them. She had loved it when Archie sat beside her on the sofa and seemed to watch them too. Sometimes she had even snuggled up to him, and once he put an arm round her shoulder. But when she turned to see if this was likely to lead to anything more he had dozed off. So perhaps it was best to watch alone.

One evening Archie came home in a black mood. He slammed the front door and kicked the umbrella stand. Molly jumped up and ran into the hall.

'Whatever is the matter Archie?'

'Bloody Bob. Money gone.'

'Money? What money?'

'Brassbound bloody money.'

Molly went pale. 'But Archie, you said he would double it - '

'Well, he didn't. Mine gone phut.' And he stumped off to bed.

At first Molly was shocked, but then she thought that after all she had been all right without it, and she and Archie were managing very well, so what did it matter?

When Archie suggested selling Balmoral and living in the boarding house which he had previously reviled, so as to invest the proceeds, Molly rebelled. She had had enough of investing. Her father had left her 'safe' shares. She had always felt he would not have approved of the Brassbound adventure and she was rather glad it was over. She certainly wasn't going to part with any 'safe' shares, and she wasn't going to move.

Archie got sullen and spent more and more time in the pub. Molly became alarmed. It seemed like the story of Emily all over again.

Coming back from the shops one day she saw Archie getting into a taxi with a couple of suitcases and she stood still in amazement. A soft cry of 'Archie' escaped her lips but the taxi was off in the opposite direction.

For a while she half expected him to telephone to explain, or to reappear, or even to write a letter. But after a week or two she accepted that he had gone and, as after her father had died, she aired all the rooms and cleaned and polished until there was no sign or smell to remind her of him. All he had left behind was a shabby raincoat, and she threw it away.

At first only the Indian newsagent was aware of any change and he was sorry. Parsley was a good lady and deserved a good man. 'Jessop not here?' he asked. Molly, open as usual, said 'Mr Jessop has gone.'

'Jessop not a good man. Parsley should find a good man or be alone.'

Molly was grateful to him for his understanding. This was what she desperately needed at the moment, and as before, when she felt totally bereft, she thought of Mrs Turtle. She knew Mrs Turtle would be rather superior about it - would have known from the first but didn't like to say anything, and so on. But she would also be strong and positive, and that was something Molly needed.

However she decided that the first thing she must do was write and tell Marjorie. This might be the ideal moment for a visit to the Bryces. She settled at her mother's little desk and searched for writing paper. She hadn't written a letter since inviting Emily to the wedding, which reminded her that she might also write to Emily. She would be sure to understand. She found some headed paper and fell to visualising her mother sitting at the desk, when they first moved in, writing little notes to cousins and friends. What had happened to them? Over the years they died or disappeared and it had seemed sad that no-one took their places, but of course they had each other and somehow their trivial lives seemed so important. Would Marjorie be in for tea? Should she and Molly go to London together for the day? Was it time to buy the bedding plants? It had seemed enough, and certainly to Molly all-absorbing.

Molly became quite excited at the thought of starting up a correspondence with Emily, but Marjorie must come first. She told Marjorie that Archie had left because he was ashamed to have lost her savings. She didn't believe it and even written down in her small, honest handwriting it looked doubtful. But everything about Archie had always been doubtful. Marjorie wouldn't know that, and she didn't want Marjorie to think too badly of him, or of her choice. In fact she was beginning to build up a picture of Archie which was a great comfort to her. He was unlucky all his life, he had been devoted to Molly but he couldn't live with his guilt over the shares. She must not pursue him, he must have his solitude. She pushed into the background the thought that such a man would one day return because she knew he wasn't really that man and would not return.

To her surprise she had a telephone call from Marjorie two days later.

'I'm sorry it didn't work out, Molly my dear. And to tell you the truth I've had as much as I can take of Roy. I'm coming home. Expect me on Tuesday.'

This Molly found more amazing than Archie leaving. Marjorie never made mistakes, and after all she and Roy had seemed quite fond of each other, and well suited. But how could you tell? Perhaps Marjorie had wanted more from Roy than Molly had from Archie. She had always stayed out later as a girl, disappeared with young men on long walks, coming home looking flushed and pleased with herself. Molly had expected Marjorie to marry, though Mother said she was too fussy. She was inclined to flick the dandruff off the young men's shoulders and straighten their ties, which Molly could see they didn't like. Perhaps that was what happened with Roy. He might have tried to relax and that would never do for Marjorie.

Emily replied at once. She was very sorry that it hadn't worked out. Archie was too much like his brother. They were totally selfish. 'I hope you had some happy times,' she wrote. 'Bernard and I did and I like to remember that.'

Marjorie returned to Balmoral the following week and soon it was as if she had never been away. She was curiously uninterested in Archie and Molly began to wonder whether he had really existed. She tried to visualise him dozing on the sofa in front of the television set. She looked at the place where he had been but she could not conjure him up. Even his voice had gone, as if he too were dead.

'Pity about Mrs Turtle,' said Marjorie. 'But I have an idea. I'll tell you about it this evening. Now we'll go shopping and have a coffee at Claytons.'

Mr Whalley reported that things at Balmoral had returned to normal and his wife raised her eyebrows and shrugged. Back to normal meant back to their dull routine. 'Just let me know when they do cartwheels down the road or come out in ball gowns, otherwise - ' and she turned back to the mirror and continued to make up her face.

The Indian newsagent greeted them warmly. 'The Parsleys - Madam and Madam Parsley,' he beamed. 'Now all is right again,' and even Marjorie couldn't be churlish enough to correct him.

At Claytons they had coffee and cakes. Molly half expected Archie to appear and wondered how she would introduce him to Marjorie. 'My husband?' That wouldn't do. Yet he wasn't an ex-husband. But perhaps he would pretend not to know her.

'Come along, Molly, eat up. Stop dreaming.'

More of a nightmare, Molly thought, but she was worrying about nothing. Archie would have moved away. He wouldn't want to bump into her and in Bournemouth they would be bound to meet in the end. On the way home Molly asked shyly 'What about Roy? I thought you were - well, fond of each other.'

'He was too fond,' said Marjorie briskly. 'Roy has no sense of timing, no sense of decorum. Night is the time for bed, daylight is for working.' And on this cryptic note she dropped the subject. Obviously Roy was the very opposite of Archie, Mollie thought. But had he pounced on Marjorie during the day, when she had merely gone upstairs to change her dress? Would he have dared? And yet - well, it was no good wondering. If Marjorie wasn't going to say any more, that was that. And there was Marjorie's idea to be discussed. Marjorie was in charge again and Molly could relax.

'You remember when we went on that cruise with the parents?' Marjorie asked, when they were both comfortably settled in the sitting room after supper.

'We were very young,' said Molly. 'I hardly remember, except that we had to play in competitions, and dress up, and I was shy. Oh, yes, they had different coloured lights all round the deck at night, and there was a smell of burning rubber because one of them was broken or something - and - '

'Yes, well that's neither here nor there. But you remember we went ashore on that island in the Pacific - Fundador?'

'Yes. It was very hot.'

'And they had English policemen. Well not actually English, but dressed like English policemen would abroad - crisp white suits and police helmets.'

'They had a parade.' Molly remembered white buildings, covered with purple flowers growing up the walls.

'Well,' said Marjorie 'that's where we're going.'

'For a holiday? What a wonderful idea.' Molly beamed at her.

'No,' said Marjorie, 'for good.'

Molly's mouth opened and shut and she blinked. 'Leave Bournemouth? Sell Balmoral?' she asked in a hushed voice.

'Of course. We'll sell up and go.'

Marjorie had come to this decision when she was packing up at Clacton. Roy had watched her, not too upset. He had found her rules and regulations hard to bear, especially when it came to bed. She was not unresponsive but everything depended on routine and it was no good even touching her if she hadn't carefully cleaned her face and pinned up her hair. And then her dressing gown had to be hung up, her slippers put in the right place. She would get into bed, take off her watch and wind it and place it on the bedside table. Roy felt as if she were starting a stop watch. He had about ten minutes to get going and half an hour altogether before Marjorie gave a satisfied sigh and put out the light. He was beginning to find the part-time typist in the office a good deal more attractive than Marjorie. And she seemed ready for advances any time he had a spare moment. It could lead to something very satisfactory, but only without Marjorie around. So although he said petulantly 'I can't understand why you're leaving me,' he really felt rather elated, and offered to pack one of her suitcases.

'Don't be absurd, Roy,' she said. 'When they're ready you can take them down to the hall. I'll send for the furniture that's mine and we'll come to some arrangement about the house.' And Molly and I will move to greener fields, she thought. Roy was a wimp. He had no business sense - no social sense - really not much sense at all. The only thing which slightly concerned her was that she had misjudged him. But *The Game of Life* ... could be relied upon to explain it. She read that in a situation like this it was obvious that she was too unselfish. She wanted him to succeed so she transferred her own abilities to him, in her mind. That he had not been able to take on this rôle was not her fault. She had given another human being a unique chance. It had been rejected, but she would be a stronger person as a result. She must be more careful in future.

Now Marjorie felt ready to shine in society in her own right - to show her mettle. But which society? They had never cultivated Bournemouth and Clacton was a dead end. No, it must be somewhere abroad, where they would be accepted at their own (or at least Marjorie's) valuation. Somewhere small. An island perhaps? Of course, Fundador.

'Yes, Molly, Fundador. You know,' she added, unusually pensive, 'we didn't make mistakes. It was all part of a plan.'

'But Marjorie, you never knew Archie - '

'Not my plan, a universal plan. These Things Happen. But they have positive results.' She had read this in a magazine, she couldn't remember which one, but it was obviously right. 'We will never be envious of married women - who knows what goes on behind the scenes - and we have a prize which helps enormously, even in this feminist age - '

'What - what?' Molly asked excitedly. What on earth could they have which was so wonderful? Trust Marjorie.

'We are both "Mrs". Mrs Bryce and Mrs Jessop, respectable women of a certain age. You'll notice people won't like to ask what happened to our husbands. We will be respectable widows.'

It was the first time Marjorie had revealed her deepest thoughts. But she had to, to be sure that Molly didn't spoil it all. Molly was so ingenuous. Now she looked shocked.

'Oh Marjorie, we couldn't - '

'Of course we won't *say* so - we won't need to. I might sigh and say "Poor Roy" occasionally. After all he is an object for pity.'

'I could never say "Poor Archie", even though he is,' said Molly.

'You won't need to say anything. In fact that's what I want you to promise. Never say a word about Archie. I will drop the necessary hints.'

'Oh dear.' Molly looked thoroughly anxious.

Marjorie said 'I won't tell a lie - don't worry.' And she thought about the way she would sigh, look soulful then shake her head as if to put away sad thoughts. She even shook her head now and Molly, looking at her, thought she did look a little sad. How clever she was. She always had been. 'Leave it all to Marjorie,' their mother had said, and that was what Molly would do.

'Now come along,' said Marjorie, 'get a note pad and pencil and we'll make a list. There's a great deal to do.'

Molly bustled happily about, collecting pad and paper, and a hard book to write on, whilst Marjorie sat up straight, ready to dictate.

Next morning a letter came addressed to Molly. This was most unusual and Marjorie studied the envelope carefully. 'It's addressed to you, Molly. The post mark is all blurred - it could be - ' But Molly couldn't wait. She snatched it from Marjorie's hand and tore open the envelope. 'Well,' said Marjorie, rather put out. She hadn't even had time to criticise the pale mauve envelope.

As Molly had suspected, it was from Emily, and she read it out to Marjorie. Emily said they had to leave the house. Although she would get half the money it wasn't enough for even a flat so she must find a full-time job. She was a bit worried about Alma. There would be the whole of the summer to get through and she couldn't be alone in some rented rooms. 'But I'm sure we'll find something and work it out. I hope you and Marjorie are well. Alma sends her love and so do I - Emily.'

Molly looked up, her face aglow. 'Oh Marjorie, let's take Alma with us for the summer! I'll pay for her. Oh do say yes. It would be good for her and - a help to us,' she added. Put that way Marjorie would be bound to be interested and she was. After a few moments thought she agreed.

'But she will be your responsibility, Molly, I can't be distracted by any childish nonsense.'

'Of course not Marjorie. I know she will be good as gold.'

'If she wants to come, remember. And if Emily agrees.'

Molly could not imagine either of them hesitating a moment. It was the perfect solution. Happily she sat at her mother's desk and wrote off to Emily. By return Emily's reply came. She was grateful, relieved, delighted - all Molly could hope for. And Alma wrote on another sheet of pale mauve paper 'Dear Aunt Molly - I can't wait. Mummy is making me a sun dress. I already have a swim suit. A stretch one so it grows with me. I like swimming, don't you? I am trying to make a sun hat.'

Emily arranged for Alma to have a term off from school. She said that one of her aunts was an ex-school teacher and would tutor Alma so she wouldn't get behind in her lessons. Again Emily was alarmed at how easy lying was. When she told Ted her parents had moved in she felt no compunction at all. And now, saying that Marjorie was a teacher, she almost believed it herself. She wondered how far one might go along this path. She thought about women who took babies in prams and passed them off as their own. People who applied for jobs saying they had qualifications to which they were not entitled. Men who committed bigamy. Lying was so easy, and eventually you believed the lies yourself.

Molly spent the last few weeks at Balmoral in a dream. She carried out Marjorie's instructions to the letter. An excited Mrs Turtle was brought back to help whenever she had a spare morning, which seemed to be fairly often. Furniture was sent to the sales or packed up for transport overseas. 'Not like the old days I don't expect,' said Marjorie. 'I remember Mother saying that when they moved to Bournemouth Carter Paterson put everything in the new house according to a plan Father had made on a piece of paper, and when they arrived the table was laid out for tea and there was jam in a glass dish.' She had imagined these great big removal men, in their white aprons, suddenly becoming perfect housewives. Setting everything out, surveying the table and nodding to each other before quietly leaving the house and locking the front door.

'Of course they laid it in the kitchen, and put out knives and forks, and everything for a big meal, but even so - '

'Why did they do that?' Molly asked.

'Molly, you're so unworldly. You know when Mrs Turtle says she's got a relative coming to tea she means a proper meal. That's what they mean by tea.'

'They, Marjorie?'

'People of that social standing. Do be sensible Molly.'

'Oh.' But Molly was doubtful. 'Then why do all those people come in at tea time at Claytons and drink tea and eat cakes? I don't think they're very grand people.'

'I can't see why you want to go on about it Molly. It's just a fact of life. Of course some people may break out of their mould, but the majority - anyway, let's get on,' and she cast an eye over the longest list Molly had ever seen in her hands.

Molly, off at Marjorie's bidding, thought perhaps Marjorie was old fashioned. Perhaps Carter Paterson men did eat enormous teas in those days, but after all, most people were the same now. And if they had tea and cakes in Claytons they could hardly go home and have another meal right away. Molly dimly saw that Fundador would probably accord with Marjorie's view of life. There would be an old fashioned social order, and they would be much nearer the top than they were in England. Marjorie would like that, and Molly would too because if Marjorie were busy in some kind of social circle Molly could escape and at last fill her time with useful work away from home. She might meet nice people and have tea, or whatever they had, with them. And there would be Alma. She must take good care of her. Life had never looked so rosy.

Emily brought Alma to them the day before they were due to leave. The house was nearly empty and what was left was to be cleared after they had gone, under the supervision of Mrs Turtle.

Alma was very self-possessed. She said good-bye to Emily without a qualm. 'Take care, Mummy. And you promised to write *every* week.'

'Of course, darling. And you be good and help your aunts as much as you can.'

'I will.'

Emily went back to Clapham, determined that before Alma returned she would have worked something out for their future.

Mr and Mrs Whalley, alerted by days of comings and goings, were at their bedroom window to watch the departure.

'Well, they're off. Heaven knows where to. And they're taking that girl with them.'

'She's the one who went to one of the weddings.'

'Must be a niece - '

'But where can they be going?'

Mr Whalley said 'You should have got talking to that woman who cleans for them. She's there on the doorstep, waving them off.'

'Too late. I can hardly go round now and ask.'

The Whalleys spent the evening speculating on what had brought about the removal of the royal family from Balmoral, their final conclusion being that a wealthy relative in the North of England had left them a mansion, and that the girl was to be trained as a junior slave to ensure that HRH should be taken care of for the rest of her days.

'I'm glad we decided to come by sea. We wouldn't have been able to bring much on a plane.' Marjorie was lying on her bed whilst Molly was searching for something in the trunk - the wonderful old wardrobe trunk belonging to their parents. 'Look in a drawer, Molly. They're bound to be there. I remember telling you to put smaller things in the drawers.'

Alma gazed in fascination at the amazing black trunk.

'It's like a cupboard,' she said.

'It *is* a cupboard,' said Marjorie proudly.

'Here you are!' Molly triumphantly held up a pair of gym shoes.

'Well done, Molly. Yes indeed, on a plane you have nothing and you're all squashed up together, with those package people.'

Alma looked at the gym shoes with interest. 'Mine are trainers,' she said.

'What are you training for?' asked Marjorie, and Alma was confused.

Molly, thinking about package tours, had perceived that some of the passengers on the boat were out of the same package, so to speak, which led to her next remark. 'It was clever of you to get us places at the purser's table, Marjorie.'

Marjorie looked complacent. 'I knew we couldn't get to the captain's table. I read an article in *The Lady* about cruising. They said it was important to be at an officer's table. Of course, the captain has all the personalities, but the purser - '

Marjorie had made sure they were almost first off the train. She marched Molly and Alma briskly across the dockside and up the gangway, Molly encumbered by two suitcases and Alma with one case and two plastic bags. They were obliged to walk up crabwise, to make room for their impedimenta, but Marjorie, who needed free hands to show tickets and passports, was soon at the top and calling to them. 'Come along, you two. Don't waste time.'

'Why do we have to hurry, Aunt Molly?' gasped Alma.

'I'm not sure, dear,' said Molly, 'but it must be right.'

A white-jacketed steward directed them to their cabin on B Deck, which contained two bunks, one above the other and a narrow bed. Marjorie pointed to the bed. 'I'll sleep there and Alma can have the top bunk over you Molly. Now I'm off to book our table in the dining room.'

She told the chief steward that on their last trip they had been at the purser's table and would like to repeat the experience. 'A previous purser, of course, but I'm sure they're all gentlemen.' She did not mention the fact that the previous trip had been over thirty years ago, and in fact it was the third officer's table. The chief steward was impressed, as Marjorie could see. She was glad not to be embarrassed by Molly and Alma who would have given the wrong impression.

She returned to the cabin exhausted and immediately lay down on the bed, where she stayed until the ship sailed, and after unpacking all they needed on the voyage Molly and Alma explored excitedly, like two children. They looked over the side, half expecting to see waving friends; they went on the boat deck and peered under the tarpaulins which covered the lifeboats, half expecting to see stowaways; they found the swimming pool, still covered, and looked under a loose rope into the pool half expecting to see a body floating as a result of a murder on the last voyage. Alma had never had such a friend.

Finally, somewhat breathless, Molly said 'Shall we go back to the cabin, to see if Marjorie needs anything?'

Alma stopped and turned. Seeing Molly's happy, pink face, she threw herself at her and hugged her. 'Dear Aunt Molly,' she said, and Molly didn't know when she had been so happy.

Marjorie felt she was accompanying two teenagers. Alma was old for her years and Molly perpetually young. They enjoyed everything, they played deck quoits and they got involved in ping-pong tournaments. When it came to swimming Molly sat and watched - she felt too fat and she couldn't swim. 'It doesn't matter if you can't swim,' Alma told her. 'It's only four strokes from one side of the pool to the other, and you can keep one foot on the bottom.' But she was perfectly happy to have Molly watch admiringly from the side of the pool.

Marjorie spent much time in the lounge reading magazines and talking to the more discerning passengers. They agreed that most of their co-passengers might as well be on a cross-channel ferry. All they seemed to want was discos and drink. However, one lounge was quieter than the rest, and there was also a library, so it was possible to find peace and quiet. Everyone had deck chairs and Marjorie had soon found a quiet spot on an upper deck, out of the wind and with only room for a very few chairs. There were one or two excursions when they called in at ports on the way, when Marjorie would take the opportunity to stroll round the empty ship and chat with any officers who might also be taking advantage of the absence of passengers.

Every so often Marjorie was asked to judge a competition, which she did impeccably. Otherwise she held herself slightly aloof and at the purser's table it was accepted that she was the important person. No-one knew quite why, but it was accepted. Until Marjorie had finished her meal no-one moved. As soon as she rose, they all rose too. It was as if she were a minor royal, or at least a senior ranking wife. Marjorie felt that at last she was entering the phase of her life for which she had been born.

By the time they reached Fundador they were all three prepared for the hot weather. Molly was quite happy to wear her sun dress, showing plump arms and legs, and to stroll about in sandals. To Alma it was second nature and Marjorie went so far as to wear a short-sleeved cotton dress and low-heeled white shoes.

Fundador appeared over the horizon very early one morning. Molly and Alma were on deck to watch the island becoming larger and larger, until they could see people moving on the dockside. Marjorie meanwhile was calculating how much should be left in tips so as to give the impression of modest affluence coupled with worldly experience. When she joined Alma and Molly on deck she was in time to see their luggage being deposited at the foot of the gangway.

Respectful passengers made way for the trio as Marjorie strode towards the gangway, and as they descended one or two murmured 'Good luck' or gave a slight wave. Marjorie had not encouraged intimacy but they admired her courage in deciding to live on Fundador - for it was obviously her decision. They might have admired Molly for agreeing to come, but they regarded her as slightly simple, and lucky to have such a determined sister.

Marjorie inclined her head slightly to right and left, raised an imperial hand to beckon to a small group of men who sat on the sea wall regarding the spectacle, and an old chap shuffled forward and piled their luggage on to a creaking barrow which might or might not have been there for the purpose. Their luggage was loaded on to the only taxi on the quayside and they were ushered inside by the smiling driver. After a few explosions from the exhaust, they set off towards the town, and the agent who would take them to their new home.

Six

Marjorie generously named their villa after both herself and Molly, but her gesture was annoyingly spoilt by the Fundadorans' insistence on putting the accent on the second syllable, some even going so far as to say it should be Marmoli, at which Molly would beam and Marjorie sniff and change the subject.

The villa was in a quiet cul-de-sac off the residential end of the main street. The shops were in the old part of town so that only the more discerning tourists bothered to carry on up to the residential end, to see what the houses were like, and few ventured along the un-named cul-de-sac. Even in summer there was a feeling of its being an oasis in the middle of a hot, dusty desert. The gardens in this road were full and green. Red and pink geraniums gave an almost permanent backing to the flowers which came and went with the barely perceptible seasons, and in the evenings the earth, profusely watered, smelled lusciously damp. A boy of about twelve would water all the gardens after school each weekday, and come to the back doors on Friday nights, holding out his cap. People gave what they felt like and he never argued, just smiled, bowed slightly and was off. 'That's how life should be,' said Marjorie. 'To each according to his needs.'

'We don't really know his needs,' said Molly, 'but I suppose it's all right. He seems happy enough.'

'Of course he is. What could he possibly spend money on here?'

Marjorie had insisted that they brought with them all that would fit into the villa. She had no desire to cover the floors with native weave rugs, to fill the house with brightly painted local furniture, or to eat off peasant pottery. This is what distinguished their house from those of other displaced British residents, and distinguished was what she meant to be. Molly would never be distinguished. She had no wish to be and never had but she was proud of the distinction which Marjorie effortlessly put into all she did. So Marjorie felt no qualms. She meant to be a big fish in a small pool and Molly would be a willing acolyte. A happy acolyte.

Now she found Molly in the kitchen making beautifully thin cucumber sandwiches. Cakes and scones were covered with muslin against the flies. Marjorie peered at them critically. 'Lovely Molly, but I think we'll give up doyleys.'

'Oh Marjorie, why? We've always used them. They're so pretty and we brought them specially.'

'I know, but I do pride myself on observation - '

'Quite rightly.'

' - and I notice that none of the best people here use them. No, they must go. You wouldn't have noticed, of course, but believe me they simply are not suitable. Now I'll just go and see that everything is quite ready in the drawing room.'

Molly still found it strange to call it the drawing room. After all neither of them had any artistic bent. Marjorie explained that it was short for withdrawing room - some article she had read in *Homes and Gardens* at the library. It fitted their new image. So Molly tried to remember.

Marjorie stopped in the hall to straighten the framed print of the Arms of Hampshire, in its dark corner by the front door, where only the most ill-bred and inquisitive visitor would dare to study its heraldic meaning. She adjusted the silver salver on the hall table, made sure the clothes brushes were placed in order of size, with the tortoiseshell shoe horn stiffly beside them. She gave the small brass gong an extra rub with a tissue, and gazed round the crowded hall.

She had brought the heavy oak stand with the mirror above it and the large brass hooks on either side for coats, and the floors were carpeted wall to wall.

She moved into the drawing room. Everything looked perfect. The pictures round the walls were scenes of the British countryside and, over the desk - their mother's little desk — were a group of silhouettes in old black frames. These Marjorie had bought in Clacton at a sale and she felt they gave an elegant touch to the room. It was a large, cool room, filled with furniture from Balmoral. The old sofa and armchairs, several odd chairs, a nest of tables, a coffee table, and a sofa table by the wall. This was now covered with cups, saucers and plates of good English design, and beside them small linen table napkins. With a nod of satisfaction Marjorie left the room, closing the door quietly. No wonder Miss Mavis Genova, from one of the best local families, said admiringly it was like visiting a museum. It was a museum. A part of England and a shining example to them all.

In the hall a slight scraping sound drew Marjorie's attention to the door which led to the patio. The wire mosquito netting frame on the outside had been quietly pulled back. Now the door itself was inching open, and it was no surprise to see the small brown face of Alma peering round it, eyes blinking after the bright sunlight outside. Her eyes focused on Marjorie and she stopped blinking. Marjorie said, quite kindly, 'Now Alma dear,

I've got important visitors for tea. I hope you won't keep popping in and out.'

'No', said Alma. 'I just wondered if I could go with Tessie to the swimming baths.'

Marjorie disapproved of Tessie even more than she disapproved of the swimming baths, but it would keep the child away from the house for a couple of hours. Tessie came from the wrong end of the town and no-one knew quite how Alma had met her. But since there were no other children in the cul-de-sac it was difficult to do anything about it. Alma thanked Marjorie and quickly disappeared, leaving only the sound of the scrape of the mosquito net frame shutting behind her, and Marjorie forgot about her at once.

Looking at her watch she decided she just had time for twenty minutes with her feet up. 'Twenty minutes, Molly,' she called, passing the kitchen.

'I'm nearly finished. Then I'll go up and powder my nose,' Molly replied. Since it had been red and shining for some time that was a good idea, thought Marjorie, but of course it meant Molly would be late, coming breathlessly into the drawing room after the last guest had arrived.

Marjorie slipped off her shoes, folded back the cellophane cover over the pink and white counterpane on her bed, then the counterpane itself, and settled herself neatly on the bed, resting her head on a special little cushion attached to the headrest. She took up *The Game of Life* ... and it fell open at a much-read page. 'So long as you know that you have done your duty - ' Her eyes took in the familiar words and she drifted into a light sleep.

Molly was not always included in Marjorie's tea parties, which she found hard to understand. She hadn't really noticed that Marjorie was becoming grander, so she couldn't know that she let down the tone of these occasions with her 'Just as it comes, dear?' and 'With or without?' Quite unnecessary, when Marjorie was there to enquire if milk were needed, in that special hushed voice which gave the impression that the words had appeared on the air without her assistance, and could be answered in the same way. She knew perfectly well that tea should be neither weak nor strong, that milk should go in last (though this point struck Marjorie as somewhat impractical), and that people helped themselves to sugar. The main object was to draw as little attention to the operation as possible; the recipient would accept the cup and saucer with a deprecating half-smile, a sound which might be taken merely for a clearing of the throat, and eyes would slide away from cup and saucer, as if to show interest in it would be to reveal some reprehensible anti-social habit. Alas, Molly was oblivious to these niceties.

The ladies who had been invited to tea today at the Villa Marmol were all concerned with the 'Save the Savage League', which planned to bring medicine, hygiene and education to the three hundred or so inhabitants of nearby Atoll Assandra, some thirty miles south of Fundador. The Assandrians had somehow managed to evade civilisation, and their island had little to offer to the outsider, yet they were perfectly self-sufficient, their needs being very basic. The island was mainly dense forest, and there was only one bay which could boast a sandy beach. It was in the forest close to this bay that the inhabitants lived. Fundadorans rarely visited the island. There was nothing for them there and the timid islanders were seldom seen. When the jungle was penetrated they hid in caves, whose entrances were almost impossible to find.

However, soon after her arrival in Fundador, Marjorie had been walking along the North Shore and had come across the body of an Assandrian, washed up by the tide. It was a nasty shock, and she had taken to her bed for twenty-four hours. Whilst lying in bed Molly came breathlessly into her room and told her that Dr Bertoli had announced that death had been due to cholera, and everyone must be inoculated against the disease. Shortly afterwards Dr Bertoli himself arrived, to give Mrs Bryce the first inoculation on the island since she had been closest to the victim. She received it bravely, and it was then that she had the inspired notion that she should form the 'Save the Savage League'. To the chagrin of various British ladies on the island Mrs Bryce had achieved a social coup, all the more annoying since she had not had to seek it, it had been thrust upon her. Naturally wherever Marjorie went she was asked about her adventure. What had the Assandrian looked like? Was it in fact a man? Did the body show signs of ravage? At this point Marjorie would move into a short speech about the League she was forming, and receive her questioner's eager support.

'A good Christian education,' said Marjorie, whose final aim was to see every Assandrian living in a fully carpeted house, drinking tea from china cups, endlessly grateful to she who had brought them to this summit of civilisation. She only regretted that they could not first become slaves, so that she could emancipate them.

Today over tea the ladies would discuss the fête which was to be held in the cul-de-sac to raise funds.

'More tea, Mrs Moravia?'

'Please. That was indeed a delicious repast. You are most kind Mrs Bryce.'

Marjorie inclined her head graciously, and poured the tea.

Miss Genova said 'It seems to me we have some good schemes for raising money. No doubt you would like me to be the Treasurer?' She was always a worker bee.

Marjorie said 'So kind of you, and Molly will help you.'

Miss Genova and Molly smiled at each other.

Mrs Galateo promised to organise a local art show, and Mrs Pardoe to get helpers for the fête. All eight houses in the road could contribute a stall. Molly would have a handiwork stall, for Villa Marmol. Mrs Pardoe cakes and sweets. Mrs Hobson-Jones bric-a-brac (she longed to get hold of some of Mrs Bryce's brass ornaments). Mrs Pardoe could vouch for the houses not represented at the tea party, despite knowing that Mrs Venables had taken a serious dislike to Mrs Bryce.

It was all very satisfactory.

'Have another eclair, Mrs Moravia? All home made. Nothing on this table I would not have had at home in England.'

'May I? How kind.'

'But of course. I know how much you all enjoy our home made cakes.'

Mrs Moravia said 'I hope we may all meet at my house next week?'

'That is very kind of you, Mrs Moravia,' said Marjorie. She did not relish the prospect of sweet-meats wrapped in tissue paper which, when unwrapped, held together until they reached your lips, where they at once disintegrated and cascaded down your chin. And the tea - well, it was a cross one had to bear. 'We will look forward to it,' she said, royally.

The sisters cleared the table after their visitors had departed, and left the debris in the kitchen. They had help in the form of a local girl, fat and smiling, who answered to the name of Matty. She and Molly took care of everything.

Matty lived in a little room above the kitchen, which she reached by sturdy wooden steps beside the back door. She could not speak English, other than to say 'Yes Mom' or 'No Mom', and no amount of effort on Mrs Bryce's part, pointing at objects, and naming them in slow, loud English, could rouse Matty's interest in the English language. She was a wonderful girl, Mrs Bryce admitted - rather proudly, in fact, since she had found her. At least, she had taken the bold step of agreeing with Matty that she should employ her.

Soon after their arrival Matty had appeared at the back door, smiling and nodding, pointing up the wooden stairs and making signs of putting her head on a pillow, and sleeping soundly; then of quickly running down the stairs, into the house, sweeping, plumping up cushions, polishing, darting up the front stairs, pulling sheets tight, covering beds, bringing out an ironing board - by then beads of perspiration stood out on her brow, and Marjorie made an unusual concession - she gave a sort of strangulated sound which could have passed for a laugh. Matty accepted it as such, and smiled more broadly than ever. An agreement without words was reached, and Matty moved in that very night, had never caused a moment's trouble, and accepted her small weekly wage with delight.

Even Marjorie was a little surprised by Matty's evident happiness with them. She remarked on this to Molly, who said comfortably 'She's got a happy disposition I expect, dear.'

'And of course it's a clean room,' said Marjorie. 'At least I suppose it is. I wonder if I should inspect it from time to time?'

'Oh no,' said Alma, who had been sitting quietly, collecting up her melon pips to make a necklace.

'Well Alma, I don't think it's for you to say - '

'No, but I mean you can't inspect, like a - a policeman!'

'Of course not, dear. Anyway, I would be a policewoman. Molly, what are we going to do about this child's education, if she stays much longer?'

Molly looked fondly at Alma. 'Miss Genova says they'll take her at the Convent in September, if she's still here. Wouldn't that be nice Alma?'

'I think it would,' said Alma. 'Tessie's going. She says it's rather strict.'

'I don't think Tessie is a good judge of these things,' said Marjorie severely. Then, returning to Matty, 'Matty's quite young, Molly. You would think she'd want friends. Well perhaps it's best not to stir things up.'

Alma privately thought that it might be the young man who climbed the wooden stairs each night, just after the Aunts went up to bed, who kept Matty smiling. He looked as if he knew plenty of jokes.

Alma never went to sleep before midnight, because her Aunts made her sleep in the afternoon. Aunt Marjorie seemed to be able to sleep at any time, but Alma wasn't used to it and the heat didn't worry her at all. Now she excused herself, and went to lay her melon seeds in the sun. After which she pulled up the onion which she had planted at the foot of the vine, to see if it had grown any larger, thought it had, and re-planted it. She thought of Tessie and the pool, but they didn't appeal to her this afternoon.

Tessie was always showing off in front of the boys, trying to dive and landing on her tummy with an alarming slap. Then Alma had to comfort her, and persuade her just to hold her nose and jump in, which Tessie felt to be extremely undignified. What Alma herself liked to do was to cup her hands and fill them with water from the pool, which she would carefully put on to the baking backs of the big boys, sunbathing on the edge. They liked this too, and she enjoyed being their handmaiden, and receiving casual thanks from Olympus. But yesterday the eldest Markham boy, whom she admired most of all, for his blond curly hair and deep blue eyes, had been unable to resist the temptation, when she was bending low over the pool, hands cupped, and a quick flip of his right foot had unbalanced her, and in she had gone, head first.

In spite of his having to pull her out, as she'd not been expecting sudden immersion and had no breath for it, Alma was deeply offended. She had dreamed of being rescued by him, but not in such ignominious circumstances. On top of everything it was the shallow end of the pool she had to be picked out of, and this was shameful indeed.

Tessie wasn't a very good comforter. Her giggle smote Alma's ears each time she surfaced. Later Tessie said how mean they were, and jumped in the deep end with

Alma several times, holding her nose in the approved style, but something had gone out of their friendship.

Alma now wandered over to the Club House, where she knew Mr Medino would give her an ice cold bottle of the local lemonade, very fizzy and with even a slight taste of lemon about it. She never tired of the anticipation which filled her mouth at the sight of the strange shaped bottle, with its rivulets of water running down the sides, and the glass marble in the mouth, which needed a hard press with her thumb to dislodge, and was followed by a stream of suddenly released bubbles, rushing into the mouth of the bottle.

Meanwhile, Molly went down to the library to help catalogue the books. There was a wonderful collection, left by various service people over the years, and some had been very neglected. Those which were damp and repairable they put on one side, those which could not be repaired on another, and those which were passable were catalogued and put up in the newly-painted shelves. The library was in the top of the Club House so that when she had done all she could for the day she was able to go downstairs for a glass of cordial. This she took on the patio with Miss Genova, who arrived from her local government job, hot and tired, at six o'clock. They sat contentedly under the banyan tree and discussed the Family Welfare Clinic, where Molly was to spend most of the next day. In the evening they would go together to the hospital. Molly loved working at the hospital. She wrote letters for those who spoke English, and she washed those who didn't.

Whilst Molly was at the library, Marjorie had been chairing a meeting of the RSPCA. This committee did not have much appeal for the Fundadorans but since it had been started by a previous Governor's wife various socially aspiring members of the community expressed a new found interest in it. They realised it was something which the British felt strongly about. For some reason they put animals above humans when it came to the crunch. The first, and as she had thought only, Chairman of the committee, Mrs Bandera, often related how, when that particular Governor died, his wife was dry-eyed at the funeral. Yet the year before, when her poodle had died, any mention of the dog would cause her eyes to fill with tears and her lips to tremble. So the ladies (certainly the men would have none of it) held meetings and discussed things like dog licences, which they knew no-one would ever buy, and someone had even brought in a cutting from a paper about Americans using 'pooper scoopers', at which the whole meeting had exploded into uncontrollable fits of laughter which kept breaking out again during the normally placid coffee time, ruining the delivery of all the best pieces of gossip. A few notes were taken at these meetings, and duly mislaid. And every summer they received invitations to the Government House Garden Party, when their President, the current Governor's wife, would enquire about the activities of the committee. Mrs Bandera would say it was all going very well, and since she was then unable to think of anything they had achieved the Governor's wife would kindly change the subject.

When Marjorie and Molly arrived on the island Marjorie knew that they should sign the visitors' book at Government House and she lost no time. On their second day in Villa Marmol Molly was told to drop everything, have a good wash and change into something respectable. There was some hesitation over whether gloves and hats were *de rigueur* but Marjorie, with her watchful social eye, had somehow gathered they were not. She and Molly walked down Main Street in a fashion well known to the Whalleys back in Bournemouth, and Marjorie led them decisively to the sentry box at the gates to Government House. 'We wish to sign the visitors' book' she announced, hardly glancing at the soldier in the box. Molly smiled nervously at him and he looked down his nose at her. 'This way Madam' he said deferentially to Marjorie, and the deed was done.

'You know Molly, if you had been here on your own I don't expect you would ever have signed the visitors' book.'

'No indeed.' Molly paused. 'Would it have mattered?'

'Probably not to you, Molly dear. But now you see we will be invited to a lunch party. And I will take the opportunity to tell them where my interests lie - of what I can do to help in the life of the island.'

'What sort of things?' Molly asked, rather surprised.

'Hospitals, animals, the elderly - in everything that gives life its quality.' In a magazine article she had read at the chiropodist before leaving Bournemouth she had been impressed by the phrase 'quality of life'. It was pleasantly vague, yet sounded important. She had also read an article about counselling, which seemed to be all the rage. Whatever catastrophe overcame people there was a trained counsellor available to 'talk through the experience', and tell people how to get over it. But Marjorie had no desire to talk anything through. She knew what people should do and they only had to ask her. If they didn't know how to cope they were poor fish anyway. So she would see that she was in a position to give people the benefit of her opinions and they could take them or leave them.

After their lunch at Government House, and a cosy chat which Marjorie had with the Governor's wife, it had somehow been impressed on Mrs Bandera that her term of office had come to an end. 'You have served tirelessly for five years, it is time you had a rest. Thank you so much,' the Governor's wife said on the telephone. So now here they were at a meeting, their new Chairman sitting at the head of the table, formalising what had been a very vague committee, with Mrs Bandera sitting, rather bemused, on Marjorie's right. 'I know that you have been a very popular Chairman of this committee, Mrs Bandera, and I can well understand your wish to stand down. You must have many other responsibilities and I am only too glad to do my bit.'

Everyone smiled and said how wonderful Mrs Bandera had been and, as she had done nothing, this pleased her. She smiled. 'It has been a pleasure, and now I am happy to serve under the Chairmanship of Mrs Bryce.'

By way of consolation, Mrs Bandera was deputed to choose a subject for consideration by a sub-committee which she would organise. Mrs Bandera thought perhaps rats would be a good subject. What should be done about the rats which came up from the harbour. They had been seen in Main Street and they were moving steadily up the road towards - well, here a hesitation was sufficient. Villa Marmol? Marjorie was slightly flummoxed. They must show compassion towards animals, but rats - ugh! It was agreed they would consider all aspects of rat life. Four ladies volunteered to join the sub-committee. They had no idea how they would set about it, or whether they were meant to have ideas on rat control or turning them into pets, but they did know they would get back to light refreshment and cosy gossip.

The committee closed its business on a note of optimism. 'Whatever the problem, we will find a way of dealing with it. Good night ladies.' And Marjorie gathered up her papers and left the ladies to tidy up and leave the school room as they had found it.

Seven

A small United Nations medical team came to Fundador, armed with cholera vaccine, with which to inoculate the Assandrians. Marjorie heard that they were coming when she was down at the library reading one of the magazines newly arrived from England. She heard Major Bigstaff telling Mrs Elland about it - and what were they doing together in the library in the middle of the morning she wondered? They had been whispering together, as befitted visitors to a library, but suddenly in a normal voice the Major had said 'The UN medical team arrives this afternoon. To inoculate the Assandrians. I've got to find them billets. Only three days, but still,' his voice lowered, 'I can say I'm still needed this evening - ' and his voice became a whisper once more.

Marjorie quietly replaced the magazine and went to the telephone box, firmly shutting the door. She rang the Governor's ADC and told him she would be delighted to put up a senior member of the UN team if that would help. He was very grateful and promised to 'let the chap in charge of them' know of her kind offer. Later that afternoon Major Bigstaff rang her at home. 'Awfully good of you, Mrs Bryce. A great help. I'll bring him round about six o'clock. Colonel Amstrad - Scandinavian - jolly good chap. They're all dining at Government House.' And shortly afterwards the ADC rang. 'The Governor and his wife are entertaining the UN team to dinner this evening. They'd be delighted if you could join them. They apologise for the short notice.'

'I quite understand. I'd be delighted,' Marjorie replied, as one who is constantly being asked to help out at Government House parties.

Molly and Alma were as thrilled as if they too were going to dine at Government House, but Marjorie soon brought them down to earth. She told them that Alma's room must be prepared for Colonel Amstrad and Alma must move into the small room at the back. 'Why can't he sleep in the back room, Aunt Molly?' Alma asked. 'I'm sure he wouldn't mind.'

But Molly said no, it would seem very strange to come from dinner at Government House to a small back bedroom.

'Sometimes in the army they live in tents,' said Alma.

'Only on manoeuvres and that sort of thing,' said Molly. 'No, we must make him feel at home.'

So the two of them removed all trace of Alma from her bedroom and made up the bed for Colonel Amstrad. Marjorie, after a short rest, which was all she had time for that day, came to see how they had got on. She approved.

'You've done a good job,' she told them. 'A small vase of flowers on the dressing table perhaps. And a clothes brush from the hall.'

'And the shoe horn?' asked Alma excitedly.

'Yes, Alma. You are a sensible girl.'

Alma lined them up on the dressing table and then went with Molly to pick the flowers.

At six o'clock Colonel Amstrad was brought along by Major Bigstaff. After the introductions Alma went to sit quietly in a corner, as she had been told to do, and studied the scene. Marjorie was at her most gracious. She was wearing a long, soft blue chiffon dress. It had been her mother's. It must have been packed away in its tissue paper for many years. But it was exactly right for Fundador. She wore long earrings, and to Alma's amazed delight she had put on a little blue eye shadow. 'She looked like a real lady,' she told Molly later.

Molly took a back seat and smiled agreeably if anyone looked her way. Major Bigstaff helped Marjorie with the drinks and Colonel Amstrad, like a cardboard cut-out in his uniform, stood at attention, from time to time bowing to one of the ladies. He was tall and fair, in his fifties, with a pleasant plump face. 'You are most kind Mrs Bryce. My work will be very easy when I have this refuge to return to.'

Forgetting herself for a moment Alma asked 'Are you a doctor?'

'Of course he is Alma. Now sit quietly,' and Marjorie dismissed her, only to be disturbed by Molly saying 'He couldn't inoculate the Assandrians if he wasn't, Alma dear.'

Marjorie turned her back on Molly and ushered the men to the two armchairs, taking her seat on the high-backed chair between them.

Colonel Amstrad felt he should be kind to the sister and the girl so he said, as he lowered himself into one of the armchairs, 'I have many years been a doctor of the elderly - geriatrica - but now I have desired to help the United Nations and must be prepared for any eventuality.'

'Like a Scout,' said Alma, admiringly.

Marjorie frowned and changed the subject. 'My father was in the Regular Army, so I am very much at home with the Services,' she said. 'My husband - ' she paused, cast her eyes down and sighed.

Major Bigstaff said 'Yes indeed' and Colonel Amstrad cleared his throat sympathetically, whilst Molly thought she just might say her husband had been in the Army, but catching Marjorie's eye she thought she might not.

When Marjorie and the officer had been swept away in the Government House car, Molly and Alma went to the kitchen for their snack supper.

'It's like Cinderella,' said Alma. 'At least there are people who go to the Ball, and people who don't, and handsome men. Well, p'raps not handsome. And they certainly aren't princes. But Aunt Marjorie did look grand, didn't she?'

'She looked pretty,' said Molly dreamily. She imagined Marjorie returning on the arm of Colonel Amstrad, gazing into his eyes. 'I wonder if he's married?'

'I expect so,' said Alma. 'Most old men are married, or else they've left their wives, so they can't be any good.'

'Alma, neither of them are old.'

'Well nearly-old,' amended Alma. 'I like nearly-old men. I might marry one one day. Of course when I'm grown up all the nearly-old men will be very old. But young ones will be getting older - '

'Come along, Alma, eat up. It's time you were in bed.'

At Government House Marjorie held forth about the 'Save the Savage League'. The Governor's wife listened with slightly glazed eyes and the UN team pondered on the British paternalistic - or in this case, they supposed, maternalistic - attitude to the aborigine.

Next morning Colonel Amstrad set out from Villa Marmol, under the glowering eyes of the rest of the cul-de-sac. Molly saw a curtain twitch and had a sudden memory of the curious eyes of their next door neighbours back in Bournemouth. In true Whalley fashion Mrs Venables asked her husband 'How does she do it? After all we've been here for fifteen years and no-one even asked us if we wanted to entertain the UN officers.'

'Did you want to entertain them my dear?'

'Well, not really, but they could have asked.'

'Perhaps she asked them. If you want something you have to go out and get it.'

'I don't really want anything. I just feel these things should be shared out. I mean, before she came everyone did something and we sort of took things easily. Now it seems like a competition.'

'What's the prize?'

'Oh, I don't know. She's in with Government House already, she can't go higher than that.'

'Then I shouldn't worry if I were you.'

'Well at least she hasn't joined the Bridge Club. That's something.'

The UN team returned from Atoll Assandra that evening with strange news. No Assandrian had any sign of cholera. Perhaps the diagnosis had been wrong? Or perhaps an epidemic was about to break out. At all events the costly and difficult operation of inoculating the Assandrians went ahead. One of the United Nations team broke a leg in a trap set outside the largest cave, but apart from this rearguard action the Assandrians were found to be a gentle tribe, extremely offended by this sudden invasion, the medical treatment and hasty departure. The team felt they had done a good job. At least the Assandrians were now entirely protected against cholera.

There was a reception for the team at the Club and, a day early, they departed.

'Your hospitality will remain a fond memory to me,' Colonel Amstrad said gallantly as he left Villa Marmol, and Marjorie, taking sole credit for his fond memories, said 'It was no trouble, Colonel. Indeed it was a pleasure. Perhaps we will see you again one day.' And Molly and Alma, in the background, smiled and murmured their goodbyes.

What a picture they made, thought Colonel Amstrad. A typical English Colonial group, a dying breed. 'Totally dead,' his team-mates assured him, but he doubted that could ever be.

Now the Assandrians had become curious. If people could come across and force their attentions on them, they had a right to repay the compliment. They started to sail across the thirty miles of treacherous sea to the main island, in boats made from scooped out tree trunks, and were found wandering in the market place, tasting fruit and throwing it away half-eaten, and naturally even had they known about payment they had nothing to pay with. They understood no-one and no-one understood them.

However, as suddenly as their visits had started they ended. People felt guilty. Those poor Assandrians had been made to feel unwanted. The fête could not come too soon. Once the money started to come in, work for the Assandrians would commence.

An effort was made to bring back the UN team to see if all was well on the atoll but this time only two of them could be mustered, and they were to stay overnight at Government House. Their tour of inspection did not last long, and Molly was the first to bring their news to Villa Marmol.

She arrived from the hospital one morning breathless from the drama of what she had to say, and the speed with which she felt it must be said.

'Oh Marjorie,' she gasped, 'It's awful - awful - '

'Pull yourself together, Molly. What is it? Now you know mother always said you shouldn't talk too fast. You'll start to hiccup in a minute.'

'Oh dear, oh dear. No, well - but it's so dreadful. Those poor Assandrians - '

'Molly, you must calm yourself. Take a deep breath and start from the beginning.'

Molly did as she was told. Alma went quite pale, watching her. 'What is it, Aunt Molly? Oh do *tell* us.'

Molly tried again. 'One of the team - one of the doctors who inoculated them - poor souls - he was a carrier. Oh, I can't bear to think of it.'

'Alma,' commanded Marjorie, 'bring me a glass.'

Alma darted away and returned with a huge tumbler. Marjorie, squinting professionally, poured into it a minute measure of brandy.

'Drink this,' she ordered, and put the glass to Molly's lips. Molly drank, gasped and eventually managed to tell her tale.

The Assandrians had all died of measles. The children of one of the members of the UN team who came to inoculate the Assandrians had measles and he must have passed it on. Since the Assandrians had never been exposed to such a virus before it had proved far more infectious to them than cholera. And also fatal.

The UN officers slipped quickly away, leaving the Fundadorans mystified. The Assandrians had never been a part of their lives and they were delighted that their consciences were no longer to be bullied about them.

If the United Nations team was upset, the 'Save the Savage League' was devastated. Alma became quite grave and downcast as her poem changed from a song of praise into a requiem. But Marjorie rallied. The RSPCA would now come into its own.

At a Coffee Morning, swiftly arranged to avoid disintegration of the rank and file, Marjorie made a dignified speech ending 'Our savages, alas, are gone. Their memory lingers on.' Alma, listening outside the window, felt that would be a good line on which to end her poem, and crept away to write it down.

Marjorie continued - 'Let us now turn to those alive - but only just. I speak of those fourth-class citizens in our little island, that abused minority - the animals! Let us turn our minds and efforts to their cause. Which of us has not seen the distress in the eyes of a dog or cat, slinking along the streets, unsure of its next meal, or from where the next foot or stone will come. Can we allow this to continue? Can we allow a fourth-class citizen in this small paradise on earth - can we?'

'No, no,' they all agreed fervently.

'People must be educated - ' said Mrs Pardoe.

'It must be possible,' said Miss Genova.

'We must all work together,' beamed Molly, and the meeting ended in joy and harmony.

A final tea was arranged for the next week, and it was agreed that this was the moment to invite the Governor's wife. It was felt that the easiest thing was for the change of cause to be indicated by the heading on the invitation card. 'To further the cause of our neglected animals,' Molly suggested, but Marjorie thought it better to be specific, and mention dogs and cats. In her heart she felt that the word 'animal' substituted for 'savage' was not sufficiently different. Anyway, she had it in mind to feature a different species each year, and she had already decided upon the donkey for special attention next year. Once the dogs and cats were fat and sleek, collared and named, the donkeys would receive her concentrated attention.

The Governor, seeing the invitation, said he had no idea Mrs Bryce was one of those.

'Well, she is now,' said his wife, philosophically, 'and as a good public servant's wife, whither the determined do-gooder goes, I follow.'

'We don't want animals tripping us up round here - you'll find yourself forced to have a cat, and it'll have to be as sleek as the sleekest on the island, and covered with bells and bows - Good God!'

To Marjorie's relief, Molly would not be present at this tea party, she and Miss Genova having been called to the hospital to help the doctors to inoculate the populace against measles. They needed much inducement, one inoculation seemed more than enough and there was a rumour that an inoculation against one disease merely gave you another.

When Molly got back to the villa, late on Saturday night, Marjorie told her what a success the tea party had been. 'A pity you weren't here, but then, you do like dashing back and forth to the hospital. Well, I'm tired. I'm going to bed.'

'Mavis and I must be up early tomorrow, dear, so I'll go to bed right away myself. Unless I can get you something?'

'No', said Marjorie. Then: 'Yes, perhaps I will have a fresh lime.' But as Molly started for the kitchen she changed her mind again. 'No, I think I'm too tired to wait for it. Thank you all the same.'

'I'm tired too,' said Molly quietly, and they went to their rooms, unusually without another word.

Once in her room Marjorie closed the door quietly and sighed, shaking her head slightly. She went through her nightly routine with deliberate thoroughness. As she creamed her face she thought she could have done with the fresh lime after all, but Molly had not been quite herself. Strange.

She got into bed and reached out for the little green book. 'So long as you have done your duty - ' she read on. And tonight she turned the page. 'Ingratitude is often a sign of jealousy.' She relaxed and closed her eyes.

The day of the fête dawned bright and clear, as most days did on the island, and by ten o'clock the stalls were out, and covered with goods for sale or raffle. The only one kept clear was Mrs Pardoe's since she must bring out her home made cakes and sweets by degrees, once the fête was open, or they would spoil in the sun. Matty had made a fan from palm leaves and had mimed how she was going to whisk it over the food stall, to keep the flies away.

Alma was in heaven. The occasion had coincided with her eighth birthday, and couldn't have been a better present, although her aunts had given her a pair of stilts, which the gardener had made, and which had the foot rests at least an inch higher than Tessie's. She had spent an hour before breakfast practising, and was now ready to take Tessie on, but both children had forgotten their stilts in the excitement of the day.

Matty gave Alma a straw hat with an enormous brim, and she wore it now, tied under her chin with a red tape. The brim bounced up and down, as she ran from stall to stall. She had copied out her poem twelve times, and even Tessie had copied it out twice, so at ten cents a copy she would make one dollar and forty cents for the cats and dogs. It wasn't quite the same as for the savages. Her heart had gone out to them, and she had woven great tales about them.

The Governor's wife had promised to look in during the morning, and when she arrived Marjorie took her from stall to stall. Dutifully she bought a little something from each. 'For my Christmas present drawer,' she said, wondering who on earth would thank her for a clump of plastic holly, a most cherished possession on this island, where such a thing had never been seen in its natural state. Someone had been very generous in parting with it, and this knowledge caused her to say, with real feeling, 'How beautiful.'

Seeing a little brown-faced girl gazing at her, her hands full of pieces of paper, she smiled kindly and asked her name.

'I'm Alma. It's my birthday. May I give you a poem?'
'Please do.'

Alma handed her a sheet of paper, slightly crumpled, and the Governor's wife read out quite loudly -

'I was a proud savage, living in a tribe,
Mrs Bryce would have helped me, if I hadn't died.
But one day we found that all of us were ill.
We fell down on the ground and lay very still.
Everyone was sad, that we had to go -

The illness was so bad, and they didn't know.
The savages alas are gone,
But their memory lingers on.
Alma Jessop. 8 yrs. exactly.'

'That's very good indeed,' said the Governor's wife. 'I hope you'll let me give you something for it, for the funds?'

'Well,' said Alma, who had been looking hard at Matty's swaying fan, and trying to pretend she was somebody else, listening to a poem she had never heard before, 'it was sort of a presentation - '

'I do appreciate it. But just because of it - not for it - I want you to take a dollar for the funds.'

Alma was thrilled, and very glad the problem had been resolved so neatly. Now she would make two dollars and thirty cents. Perhaps she would use the thirty cents on a present for Aunt Molly.

The Governor's wife was presented by Marjorie with a sleek black cat. It was wearing a smart red collar on which was a brass disk engraved with the words 'Government House'. Gratitude and pleasure were duly expressed, and the chauffeur carried it to the car. Later on in the day he returned bearing a small embroidered footstool which was auctioned, and brought the proceedings to a close.

Marjorie made a speech, thanking everyone for coming, and the helpers for their help, and ended with a few dramatic words on animal welfare. Everyone clapped, and Miss Genova started up 'For she's a jolly good fellow'. It was the first time Marjorie had ever been referred to as a fellow, or even as 'jolly good', and she took it in good part as, bowing from side to side, she made her way back to Villa Marmol.

After the street had been cleared Alma and Tessie roved around, finding useful oddments to be picked up reverently out of the dirt, cleaned and used for their own special purposes. Matty had enjoyed it all so much she was now sitting on her wooden steps, in the dusk, looking at a book of comics which Alma had given her. It was almost too dark to see, but she was chuckling and heaving back and forth appreciatively.

In the Villa Marmol Marjorie was supervising Molly in laying out the money and accounting equipment on the dining room table.

'A newspaper first. That's it. Now nothing can scratch the table. The big box nearest to you, I should think, then the smaller ones. You'll find another pencil in the bureau drawer - there, that's it. And here comes Mavis - will you answer the door, Molly?'

Marjorie stood in the hall, while Molly let in Mavis Genova.

'You did splendidly,' Marjorie told Mavis. 'Absolutely first class. I really am most grateful.'

Mavis and Molly looked pleased. 'I am grateful for the trust you put in me,' said Mavis, and she and Molly settled down at the table.

'Well,' said Marjorie, 'I won't delay you. I'll just have a little rest before dinner.'

'A good idea,' said Mavis. 'Now, Molly, we'd better get on. I've promised to help Dr Merino tomorrow, and I know you're going to a meeting of the Old Age Pensioners' Unit, so we'll have to get finished tonight.'

Marjorie left them to it, and walked upstairs to her bedroom. Really, she always managed to choose such good helpers. Molly, of course, was always reliable, but Miss Genova was a real find.

Needless to say the fête made an excellent profit, and, added to the money from the Art Show, it was possible to build an animal shelter for strays, and Molly and Mavis Genova found voluntary helpers to staff it, and sat in it themselves when there was no-one available. Behind the shelter they laid out a pets' graveyard, and almost immediately it was put to use, displaying several small marble slabs, appropriately engraved.

The islanders were amazed by all this. They knew you must look after your donkeys and goats - they were no use to you if they weren't fit. But what use were dogs and cats? Yet in a way they enjoyed the madness of it. The English were such an eccentric people. The pets' graveyard became quite a Sunday outing for the people of the island, the words on new headstones being translated by the better educated among them, and the sentiments much admired, however misplaced.

Marjorie insisted on their taking in a stray dog at the villa and was very strict about its feeding and grooming. Matty became quite competent as a kennel maid, which she took as a huge joke, and Molly made sure it got its proper exercise. It was a mongrel bitch. She looked like no other dog anyone had ever seen - a rare breed, Marjorie would say - and as time went by she took on Marjorie's bearing, and her poodle ancestry became apparent; she walked proudly, head held high. She liked to be waited on. She liked her little nap. And if Molly was too long in the bathroom or getting ready to go out, she would make her displeasure felt. They called her Belle.

Returning to Villa Marmol one afternoon Molly found Alma gazing into the magnolia bush.

'Alma dear, what are you doing?'

Without looking round Alma said, 'Counting the leaves.' Molly felt this to be an excellent answer. Counting leaves would surely keep one occupied for quite some time. Not that Alma ever bothered them with the usual child's question 'What shall I do?' She was in fact a more ideal child than Marjorie and Molly, with their lack of experience, realised.

'Dear child,' thought Molly. And also 'poor child', since they didn't really know what was to happen to her.

Molly let herself into the villa and Alma watched her rather shapeless form melting into the dark, cool hall.

Alma sighed. How wonderful it was to be left to do as she liked. She adored her aunts for not worrying about her, and half the time not remembering her. They would remember her from time to time, but only to ask, most politely, if she were all right. Aunt Marjorie didn't like Tessie, but even that she forgot until she heard the name, or saw the child.

So Alma led her private life, watched people, or watched them watching each other. When she chose to she entered a scene, took a small part, and made her quiet exit.

In the villa, Marjorie was resting, and not for the first time Molly wondered whether rest had anything to do with intellect. If she rested more would she be good at organising, like Marjorie was? She owed everything to Marjorie.

Marjorie's voice called out 'Is that you Molly?'

'Yes dear,' answered Molly, 'can I get you something?'

Marjorie's door opened and she stood there, looking elegant, hair perfectly groomed. 'Yes, do bring me an iced lime and soda - fresh limes.'

'Of course dear,' and Molly, her hair wisping round her plump pink face, trotted off towards the kitchen.

They had an old fashioned ice box in the larder, with a large block of ice in it, which fascinated Molly as much as it did young Alma. It had a strange, not unpleasant smell to it, a cross between a cool cellar and the zinc tray on which the ice stood. Ice was delivered daily in a donkey-drawn cart, melted ice dripping off the back of it, and the block which reached them must have been very large indeed when it started out. Sometimes it was still big enough to be hacked in two by the ice man, and shared with Mrs Pardoe.

There was no very good reason why they should have electric light on the island and yet no refrigerators or electric stoves. It seemed to be a local superstition that food must be kept on a block of ice and cooked over a naked flame. The sisters enjoyed it since it made them feel like pioneers, and cooking, or at least directing cooking, was Marjorie's only descent to what might be described as domestic chores. She knew just how Molly should use the flames which Matty so skilfully fanned and fed.

Molly now filled a glass from the jug of cold water in the ice box, cut and squeezed a lime, added sugar syrup, and went up to Marjorie who was sitting at her dressing table, pencilling in a neat eye-brow. She thanked her sister and took a sip from the glass. 'I can't think how we managed without fresh limes in Bournemouth,' she said, grimacing slightly as she swallowed. 'It could have done with a touch more syrup, Molly.'

'Oh dear. Give it to me. I'll take it down and put some more in,' said Molly anxiously.

'No, no. It's quite all right for this once. You know I'm not one to make other people run unnecessary errands. I'm sure you'll remember next time.'

'I will dear. I am sorry.'

'How did your meeting go? Pensioners, wasn't it?'

'We had rather bad news. Poor Mrs Ortego - she's the Chief Minister's wife - '

'I know,' said Marjorie, unimpressed.

'Well, she's in hospital. Her duodenal ulcer. She had just had lunch - and she really enjoyed it - and then - '

'Yes, Molly, I don't think we need the details. So you've lost your Chairman?'

'Not lost really. Just mislaid - I mean, for a while - '

'I quite understand.' Marjorie paused. 'Molly, have a word with your fellow committee members. It they wish it I am willing to take over in the interim.'

'Oh Marjorie, would you?'

'Of course, my dear. It's the least I can do.'

'But the RSPCA?'

'I'll manage. Where there's a will - '

'I'm sure they'll be *very* grateful.'

'Yes, I'm sure they will. Let me know the date of the next meeting. There's the Hospital Committee on Monday, but otherwise next week is fairly free.'

A delighted OAP Committee welcomed Marjorie on the following Wednesday evening in the round room at the library.

'Now ladies, tell me what are your plans for the year?'

The ladies vied with each other to impress Marjorie with their ideas. Miss Genova said she had been thinking of a Saturday Club. OAPs would be collected by members in their cars and brought to the library. They could see a video and have tea.

Marjorie, thinking of herself in ten years' time, said: 'Some of the over-sixties are highly intelligent. After all, think of the Queen. No point in thinking they just have to be kept occupied with chit-chat and cups of tea. You should arrange lectures on the history of the area - the flora and fauna - '

Miss Genova was impressed. 'We will certainly arrange lectures.'

Mention of the Queen had galvanised them all into action. Ideas were popping up from every direction, ending with Mrs Enrico suggesting an amateur dramatic society or even a band. Who knew what instruments the OAPs might be expert at. And why call them OAPs anyway? They were retired people. Why not change the name of the Committee to the Retired Persons' Club? Molly, enthusing over each new idea, thought to herself that Marjorie certainly knew how to get the best out of people. She was a real leader. Without her, nothing would change in a million years. How strange it was that Marjorie had been content to stay at home merely organising the family for all those years. Perhaps she saw the Fundadorans as one large family, needing knocking into shape.

Marjorie returned to Villa Marmol for a well-earned rest. No need for *The Game of Life* ..., she felt she had almost mastered *How to Play It*.

'Your sister's a marvel,' said Miss Genova, and Molly agreed.

At the villa, Marjorie lay on her bed, satisfied by a job well done - as usual. She pondered. Yes, she had made her mark on the leaders of local society, but what about the British - the ex-pats as she had seen them called in an article in last month's *Woman's Journal*. Only those in the cul-de-sac appreciated her, because of the fête, but even here she had noticed a little jealousy. This was inevitable and so long as it was mingled with respect she did not mind. It wasn't friends she was after, it was power. She must go further afield. Perhaps *The Game of Life* ... would help after all. Relaxing, she grasped the small green book.

Eight

Mrs Ellingworth, who had lived in Fundador for many years, seemed to feel she was a natural leader of society because she ran the Bridge Club. She had recently asked club members in a sharp, loud voice: 'Who *is* this Mrs Bryce who seems to be getting into everything? Not that these committees amount to much. Gossip shops I call them. Where did she come from?'

'Bournemouth,' said someone, pleased to have some information.

'Bournemouth,' repeated Mrs Ellingworth, much as Dame Edith Evans had been wont to say 'handbag'. Perhaps the airwaves took over these remarks and wafted them up to the Villa Marmol for it was soon after that Marjorie began to wonder about the Bridge Club. She had been in the library one day when a loud voice from the balcony called down to the cackling ladies in the patio below 'A little less noise please, we are playing Bridge.' There was a sudden silence. 'The General,' said one of the cacklers, which caused a quiet ripple of laughter. But from then on voices were lowered respectfully. And Marjorie determined to win that respect.

As a family they had played Bridge, until Marjorie had finally upset their parents by endlessly questioning their bidding, and having post-mortems. When it became obvious that she was always to be right, and that her own bidding and play was never to be investigated, enthusiasm for the game waned. Eventually their father said that he was getting too deaf to hear the bidding, and their mother said the arthritis in her fingers made it hard to hold the cards, so the cards were put away and the pads and pencils discarded. Molly had not minded being criticised, she was so used to it, and really she paid very little attention. She was sure it was well deserved, but never had any ambition to improve. Perhaps Marjorie's strictures were a form of security, since they penetrated into all parts of Molly's life. Marjorie could not forget her if she was always having to put her on the right track. But since Marjorie had accepted that the parents, however keen, were just not able to play any more then Molly had been agreeable.

Thinking it over Marjorie decided that she must brush up her Bridge before approaching Mrs Ellingworth. She ordered an Autobridge pack she saw advertised in a magazine and she wrote to Foyles for a good book on the game. They advised one by Terrence Reese and one by A F Truscott, both of which she ordered. She had tried the library at the club but they only had one book, which the librarian said had come in with a bundle of books from the home of someone who had died. It was called *The Art of Coarse Bridge*.

'Hardly suitable,' said Marjorie, who had no more desire to be coarse at the Bridge table than elsewhere, but the librarian said she had read it and it was funny.

'Funny? But Bridge is a serious game,' said Marjorie reprovingly.

'Well, it's about how people get one up on each other when they make mistakes - that kind of thing.'

'One up?' repeated Marjorie, like a Judge on the Bench querying some modern term tossed into Court by a Barrister.

'Well, you know, if you make a mistake and you're clever you can get out of it by suggesting someone else is wrong,' and the librarian laughed comfortably at the thought.

'I pride myself on never making mistakes,' said Marjorie, taking the book nevertheless.

The librarian decided not to be so helpful in future, and brought the date stamp down with a bang in the appropriate space on the fly leaf.

In bed that night Marjorie read parts of the book, with a disapproving frown, her mind however storing away one or two points for use in the unlikely event that she found herself 'one down'.

A couple of weeks of practising on the Autobridge, and reading Reese and Truscott, and she was ready to face the Bridge Club. She had always been good at cramming.

She rang Mrs Ellingworth. 'I don't believe we've met, Mrs Ellingworth. I am Mrs Bryce, from Villa Marmol.'

'Indeed we have not. I lead a very busy life here - '

'I quite understand. I just wanted to put myself forward for the Bridge Club. I believe you run it.'

'I am the organiser, yes, for my sins, but I'm afraid our standards are rather high.'

'I'm so glad. Sometimes in these places competition is so lacking that one has to put up with second best,' said Marjorie, as if she had spent her life in overseas posts, prostituting her talents to help the common weal.

Mrs Ellingworth thought quickly. 'We have to maintain our standards, Mrs Bryce. I am sure you will understand that. Perhaps you would like to come along one afternoon and see how you get on. You won't mind if we conclude that this is one opening on Fundador which does not suit your talents? And of course there is always the Mah Jong Club.'

Marjorie understood perfectly, and it was agreed that she would play the next Thursday afternoon.

On Thursday morning she visited 'Hair Magic' and Tina made a good job of her hair - a kind of mini beehive - and she turned up at the Club looking smart and formidable. Mrs Ellingworth was condescending and cool. Introductions were made, cards cut and tables arranged.

Marjorie found herself partnering a small, elderly lady, Mrs Lark, with wisping grey hair and a nervous manner. She glanced at Marjorie and away again. Mrs McArthur, plump, blonde and over-dressed, partnering Mrs Jennings, a severe lady in black, made up the foursome. There was little talk, and an atmosphere of competition prevailed. Mrs Lark had retired to Fundador with her husband some years ago. Like most of those present (there were three tables) she felt some unreasonable resentment against Marjorie. It was rather like a new pupil at school, arriving after term had begun. Everyone eyed her and no-one seemed to wish to be seen to be friendly. This suited Marjorie admirably. She had no wish to enter into pointless conversation and she was looking forward to the game. She remembered now how much she enjoyed the family games, before the family became so tiresomely sensitive. She would keep that in mind. Not everyone was open to helpful criticism.

There were two men present, both looking slightly cowed and under control. Marjorie recognised one whom she had seen in the local general store. He would stand vaguely at the counter, asking for unspecified quantities of not exactly specified commodities, and would end up taking away a heavy carton of extra large boxes of soap powder, or Vim, or enormous tins of biscuits. He would hand over his purse so that the embarrassed salesgirl could help herself. He looked the other way. It was all too horrible to contemplate, this commercialism. It was said that he had tried to barter with the Assandrians, stating that this was the proper way to live, but they had misunderstood and merely took what he offered and gave him nothing in return. It was also said (he was the victim of much good-natured gossip when there was nothing better to talk about) that he came to the island because it had only two examples of the internal combustion engine - the Governor's car and a taxi. In England he had taken to beating cars with his walking stick. His name was Eustace Proctor.

The players exchanged some information on conventions and Mrs Lark said 'We usually play the strong no trump.'

Marjorie looked down her nose. 'Oh, I see - '

'Is that all right for you?'

'Of course. After all this is not Acol Road - when in Rome - ' and she gave one of her rare and rather alarming chuckles. The room fell silent and she was conscious of eleven pairs of eyes on her.

'Variable hearts - um - ' Marjorie seemed to be speaking to herself and her now rather nervous partner decided to ignore this comment, which she did not understand.

By now their opponents, and her partner, had become slightly uneasy. Mrs Ellingworth was relying on them to put Mrs Bryce in her place, but she seemed so very confident.

Quiet questions and answers started up again at the other tables and finally the games commenced.

Mrs Lark led a four of hearts and Marjorie played the three. Holding the King and two she remembered from her reading that when leading your partner's suit from King the low card is conventional. A F Truscott had been specific and she rather thought Terrence Reese confirmed this.

Her partner took the trick with the Ace, and assuming Marjorie did not hold the King, changed the suit. A few tricks later Marjorie played her King on another heart lead, and it was trumped by their opponents. Marjorie's partner did not look pleased. When the hand was finished she asked Marjorie a little sarcastically, not to say triumphantly, in her double rôle as partner and enemy, if she had never heard of the somewhat elementary rule that she should lead the highest card of the suit called by her partner.

'No doubt you have read A F Truscott - as you know, a British International player?' Marjorie queried.

Mrs Lark looked uncomfortable but Mrs McArthur was more intrepid.

'I do not quite recall - perhaps you could quote, Mrs Bryce?' Her friends looked at her with surprised admiration. They had never heard her to be so pompous. They looked at Marjorie. Surely she could not actually quote the extract?

Marjorie started to shuffle the cards. It was noticed that she did this in a very ordinary fashion - they had half expected that she would hold them in one hand and catch them in the other.

By some blissful chance Marjorie had learned by heart the point in question.

'Indeed I do,' she finally said. During the long pause she had placed the cards neatly before the person on her right, for cutting. Now she leaned back in her chair and looked at the ceiling. 'Let me see - yes - ' she brought her gaze down and, looking Mrs Lark in the eye, she said 'To quote A F Truscott 'It is a popular fallacy that you should always lead the highest card of your partner's suit. From a holding such as King XX it is definitely a mistake to lead the King, and the bottom card should be led'; and Terrence Reese concurs.'

Mrs Lark was transfixed and unable to look away. Kindly, Marjorie turned to Mrs McArthur. 'You remember no doubt?' Mrs McArthur said gruffly 'Yes, yes. These things slip one's mind from time to time.'

There was silence as the cards were dealt, everyone watching them carefully as if they expected some sleight of hand.

All went smoothly for a while but Marjorie felt she should consolidate her position before the end of the rubber. She remembered in the *Coarse* book mention of the 'so-called Herbert negative'. Was it serious? She would chance it.

'I often think the Herbert negative is an imaginative convention,' she said, causing Mrs Lark, who was dealing, to drop a card face upwards on the table. Whilst this disaster was being sorted out Marjorie continued: 'Not many people know of it - at the Portland - but probably you know it?' she asked turning to an alarmed Mrs Jennings.

All three ladies gazed at her glassily. The fight had gone out of them. Mrs Lark said faintly 'Perhaps another time?'

'Of course.' By this time Marjorie herself was somewhat exhausted by her efforts. There was 'The Roman Club' she mused, but being unable to remember what it was she was content to call it a day and play her usual average game.

Her opponents were so flustered that they made a number of errors and they could only be grateful that Marjorie made the odd slip. They almost felt she did it to keep them in countenance, despite the fact that every little slip was explained away by some mystifying comment such as 'flexible, of course'.

From the other side of the room this had been observed and noted by Mrs Ellingworth. She had become aware that Mrs Bryce was an opponent of her own mettle and she instantly decided that her best defence was an alliance. It would be no good trying to convince the members that Mrs Bryce's skills were less than theirs. Better to welcome her and share a leading rôle.

From then on Marjorie was a part of the ex-pat society, and an invitation to their gatherings guaranteed.

Marjorie's esteem with her local committees escalated and Molly was delighted. She felt that Marjorie had achieved her aim and would now be able to rest content and, like Alma, Molly was grateful to be left alone to pursue her own interests. Her support now came from her new friends and she could manage without so much direction from above.

On the occasions when Marjorie took Belle out with her she found that people glanced at them admiringly. When out with Molly, Belle would scamper ahead and have to be called back. She would dart into shops and snuffle about in corners, or chase the odd cat. But when she went out with Marjorie she walked slightly behind her, and never gave any trouble. Marjorie took this as natural since everyone always behaved as she wished and after a while she felt something was missing if Belle was not with her. She began to take her to meetings, where she sat quietly on a cushion which Marjorie brought with her. And since she was so good Marjorie took her to the Bridge Club. This caused quite a stir since one or two people owned small dogs and had never dared to bring them along. However Marjorie came early one afternoon and by the time the rest of the players arrived Belle was sitting on her cushion and didn't even give a growl as the new arrivals took their places.

Mrs Ellingworth broached the subject. 'I see you have brought your dog, Mrs Bryce. This is not customary.'

'Oh I'm so sorry, I checked the book of rules most carefully. There is no mention of a ban on pets. And of course Belle will behave impeccably.'

Everyone knew this would be true, and they also knew that those of them who owned dogs could not vouch for them in this way. Nothing more was said. As usual Marjorie had got her way.

Molly told Alma about the dog next door to them when they were children and how it had quite easily learned to do things, so she and Alma got Belle to carry a small straw basket round the garden, and sometimes she would fetch her lead - although she would only ever allow Marjorie to attach it to her collar. They even got her to stand on her hind legs on the command: 'The Queen!'

There were no real seasons on the island. Alma had arrived at the end of the spring rains, and now it would be almost winter in England. Her mother wrote to Molly to tell her she had found a flat in London, and got herself a good job. There was a popular school nearby which was willing to take Alma, and she had a lot of catching up to do. So at last Alma was packing. Molly was helping her, and trying to make both of them feel that it was a good thing for Alma to be going home again.

Alma wasn't quite sure. She had had a nightmare the previous night, dreaming she was a block of ice, with a crack down her back. Molly said it was probably because she ate too much melon, and then Alma remembered seeing the melon on the ice in the ice box, which made them both feel better. But Alma, ever thoughtful, wondered whether it meant that she was being cut in two, part of her wanting to remain in Fundador and part of her wanting to be at home.

That evening when the house was still, after Matty's friend had crept up the wooden steps, and Belle was curled up asleep in her basket outside Marjorie's door, Alma gazed out of her window for the last time. She saw the tops of the pine trees, and memorised their swaying, pointed pattern on the sky. She listened to the distant waves on the shore, and she breathed in the night scents, dry pine needles, damp garden earth, blossom and leaf - all combined with the slightly acrid smell of native cooking coming from the Pardoe kitchen.

It was a sad day for Molly when she took Alma down to the docks. The ship was too large to come alongside and they had to go out to it in a tender. Amos, the taxi driver, knew Alma well from her visits to Tessie's part of town. Tessie was now going to the Convent and she had become quite prim. Marjorie said good-bye at the door of the villa, giving Alma a peck on the cheek and a quick wave before shutting the door. Amos and Tessie waved from the dockside, and Molly went on board with Alma. The Bradleys were going home on leave - he worked at the bank - and they had promised to keep an eye on Alma. The purser was to make sure she was handed over to Emily at the other end. There was nothing to be worried about. Molly wasn't worried, just desperately sad. But she managed to hold back her tears. Alma was so excited now at the thought of seeing Emily again that her torn emotions over her departure had faded. She felt she was in a dream. She hugged Molly. 'You've been wonderful to me, Aunt Molly. You're a true friend,' and Molly was touched to the heart.

'Good-bye Alma dear.' Then, inspired, she said: 'You must come again next year. Yes, that's it! Come with your mother.'

'Do you think we can afford it?' Alma was very conscious of their money problems.

'We'll all help,' said Molly, and her heart lifted at the thought. It would mean something to look forward to.

The cry went up 'All ashore that's going ashore' and Molly, with one last hug, left Alma and clambered back down the gangway and on to the tender. Alma watched her go, and they waved to each other until Molly could no longer make her out on the deck. On the dockside they could none of them see Alma, but they waved all the same. The liner hooted three times and slowly sailed away. Amos and Molly wiped their eyes, and Tessie went home.

Molly's feeling of desolation was so much lessened by the thought of Emily and Alma returning the next year that she was soon able to get back into her routine, and there was always some rumour or another on the island to keep everyone guessing. Mavis Genova said that since Molly and Marjorie had arrived it had been nothing but change. They were, she said grandly, catalysts.

'Are we?' said Molly dubiously, not quite sure what this meant. It couldn't be bad since Mavis' eyes shone as she said it, and she looked at Molly proudly. 'Before you came we knew nothing about the Assandrians, and now we have learned about them and they have completely gone. And we have the pets' cemetery, and all the ideas your sister gives us - oh, it is most exciting. And now this!'

'What?'

'Have you not heard? I thought most surely your sister would have had some rumour at the Bridge Club.' Mavis, like all the Fundadorans, felt that Marjorie had made the grade when she was accepted by the Bridge Club, and they regarded that club as the fount of all serious rumour. 'Why, they say that a hotel will be built on the North Shore.'

Wherever Molly went the talk was all of the hotel. It would be fifty stories high; it would have a thousand bedrooms; it would have a ballroom, a discotheque, a beauty salon, a shopping complex. There was no end to what this hotel would have. No-one bothered to wonder who would use all these facilities.

When Molly questioned Marjorie she found that the Bridge Club *had* heard the rumour but decided to wait and see. Marjorie had advised caution since she was not too happy at the idea, and really it might not be true, but if everyone talked about it it might come true. She thought that probably one of the guest houses was to be improved and enlarged.

Molly was quite disappointed. 'I expect you're right, Marjorie. You always are. But it would have been rather nice to have a hotel.'

'Why?'

'I don't know - I mean, well people could meet there - and people on cruise ships could stay and take the next ship home.'

'And that's about it,' said Marjorie dismissively.

They were shocked the following day when they received a phone call from Colonel Amstrad in Copenhagen. He was visiting Fundador on business the following week and wondered whether they could book him into a guest house. Marjorie at once said she would be delighted to put him up and he was easily persuaded. Molly, who had answered the phone and handed it over to Marjorie, quite unable to talk to anyone over such a distance - what *would* Father have said? - was in a fever for the call to end. Marjorie, once she had got used to the idea of money being thrown away in this fashion (after all, it wasn't her money) soon got into the swing and told him it was very hot - unusually so for the time of the year the locals said - and that there was a rumour of a hotel being built on the island.

'I can tell you more of that when I see you,' said Colonel Amstrad. 'My grateful thanks. Hasta bientôt!' The UN had obviously made its impact upon him.

'Well,' said Marjorie. Then she hesitated. If she told Molly that the Colonel had something to do with the hotel it might get out and Marjorie wanted to be the first with any concrete news. She must think it out. It was not quite the sort of problem which a quick perusal of *The Game of Life* ... could solve. She told Molly that the Colonel was coming to stay and they must get Alma's room ready for him. Molly was only too happy to get to work. Marjorie let it drop here and there that he was coming on a visit. He had liked it so much that he longed for a quiet week there, no entertainment, just a relaxed time at Villa Marmol.

There were two schools of thought, both on the same lines. One was that he had taken to Marjorie, the other that he had fallen for Molly. The first view was taken by Molly's circle, since knowing Molly they were aware that it would be patently obvious if anything like that was in the wind. And anyway, like themselves, such romantic adventures were not to be expected. They would get enormous vicarious pleasure if Marjorie were the one. Marjorie's acquaintances, always wary, were determined Marjorie should not improve her status yet further. It would be unbearable. And adopting her dictum that if you refused to consider something possible it would not happen, they did just that. In fact they made doubly certain, they felt, by telling each other he was obviously after Molly.

Colonel Amstrad had flown to the mainland and came over to Fundador on the steamer which made its sedate voyage there and back once a week. The four-hour voyage gave him time to get into a Fundadoran frame of mind, and clothing to suit the climate. He also had time to write a letter to his wife.

Once settled into Villa Marmol Colonel Amstrad excused himself and disappeared into the town, returning for lunch.

'Would it be over-rude of me should I make a further visit to the town today? It will then be possible for me to explain to you why I am here. I have two more important meetings and then it will be clear.'

Marjorie was eager to hear his news and very willing that he should get everything settled. She was now sure it was he who was hoping to build a hotel. He must have been in touch already with the authorities, which would be where the rumour had sprung from. After all, everyone had a relation working for the city authority in some capacity. Molly was not at home when the Colonel arrived and was mystified at lunch time when he mentioned explaining his reason for coming back to Fundador.

Marjorie said she had no idea, but if Molly got back in time for tea she could hear the news from the Colonel's lips.

Molly made sure to be back by four o'clock. She told Sally Merino, with whom she was working at the hospital, that she must get back as they had a guest.

'It's the Colonel from the United Nations, isn't it?' Sally asked.

'Yes, he's come for a rest,' said Molly, innocently, and Sally gave her a conspiratorial smile, which Molly could not understand.

'Your sister is very restful, I expect,' she said, still smiling.

'Of course,' said Molly. 'I hope we both are.' And she left for home and news.

The Colonel's first remarks were very welcome. 'I would be honoured if you would call me by my first name, and if I may take the same liberty?'

'Most certainly,' said Marjorie.

'I am Jens. My wife's name is Astrid.'

His second remark was less welcome, but not hard to come to terms with since neither sister had really entertained thoughts of a romantic interest in his direction.

'She is a charming lady and you will like her,' he went on. 'She will visit later on. And now I will tell you my news. I am to build a hotel on Fundador!'

'On the North Shore? Oh, I'm so glad it is you.'

'You knew about it? I feel most stupid. I had no idea that my secret was known to everyone.'

'Not to everyone,' said Marjorie. 'In fact the rumour was too absurd to be believed. People were saying there was to be a hotel like a Hong Kong skyscraper, and it would have more facilities than the whole of that city thrown together! Imagine, on Fundador.' She sniffed disapprovingly.

Jens laughed. 'The matter has been under discussion at private meetings, there was bound to be talk I suppose. I was lucky - a representative - Mr Tonado was, as they say, very supportive. He spoke for me all the time.'

He was glad that the rumour was so extravagant and he could at least be the first with the news that it was to be a modest hotel, some eight stories high, and with only the normal facilities. It might have a small swimming pool on the roof, but if the bay could be made safe then that would not be necessary. He brought out all the papers and plans and laid them before the sisters.

'I have no problem in getting the finance,' he said, 'but I wondered whether you might like to have a share - a stake - in it? You may see the bank manager to ensure that I am a safe person.'

Molly laughed. She had experience of unsafe people and she felt sure that Jens was safe. Marjorie also felt sure of him, but she thought it was a good idea to see the bank manager. They would have to arrange their investment through the bank in any event.

Marjorie swore Molly to secrecy until everything was signed and sealed, and until she had herself informed the Bridge Club. This she did at their meeting two days later.

'Jens is to build a small hotel on the North Shore,' she said when they were all settled at their tables. 'It's all arranged, and Molly and I have invested in it. I will be here to oversee the work when Jens is at home, and he and his wife will come to stay as soon as the first bedroom is ready. Of course, he will come from time to time before then, but he said he felt I would take care of the details better than anyone else.' She had been about to say 'on the island' but thought better of it.

The Bridge Club were agog. First there was the fact that Marjorie and the Colonel were on Christian name terms, and then the relief that this did not have too much significance since he had a wife after all. Then there was the satisfaction that the hotel was not to be a monster; and lastly the fact, which needed much chewing over, that Marjorie and Molly had invested in it and Marjorie would be keeping an eye on things.

'I expect she'll have that sister running about finding out about materials, what's happened to the furniture, when the lamps will arrive, how long before the carpets turn up - poor woman. But she seems to like it. I'm sure if Mrs Bryce told her to take a swim in North Shore Bay to make sure it was safe she would do it.'

Mrs Venables was in full spate and her husband, as usual, hid behind the paper and let out an occasional 'Yes, dear, I expect you're right.'

And of course she was. Molly was to be seen running about the town, trotting round to the North Shore and back, puffing into the hospital, running to the Retirement Club meetings. Never these days was she found in pleasant conversation with Mavis under the banyan tree in the Club gardens.

The Governor's wife was somewhat nonplussed by the turn of events. Really had her husband not been appointed by the Queen she would have felt that her own position on the island was threatened. Although she and her husband had led an exemplary Naval life before coming to Fundador, seldom pulling rank, three years on Fundador had slightly gone to their heads. If someone were asked to lunch, at however short notice, it was taken rather badly if they said they had another engagement. Dinner was an even worse hazard. Poor Mrs Hobson-Jones had a dinner party arranged when she received a last minute invitation to dine at Government House. Without delay she delivered by hand a formal regret and she and her husband had never again been invited. The Governor's wife used to refer to them, to her husband, as 'That rude couple - what's their name?' They had to be invited to the Garden Party in the summer, as every ex-pat resident was, but somehow neither the Governor nor his wife had a word with them, however busily they manoeuvred themselves into the imperial path.

Marjorie was something else. 'I must admit she is an asset,' the Governor's wife said. 'I know she is maddening, and that compared with her sister she's a bit of a monster, but she does get things done and so far without over-stepping the mark.'

'She certainly knows what she wants,' the Governor replied. 'She got Colonel Amstrad up to their place before most people even knew the UN team were arriving.'

'And now she's got in on the hotel! Well, I suppose we should encourage her.'

'I'm seeing to that,' her husband said.

'You dark horse!'

'Well you know how difficult it is finding anyone new to put forward for the Honours List. She's a godsend.'

Nine

The award of an MBE to Marjorie came as an enormous surprise to everyone on Fundador, not least Molly. Marjorie had known in advance - after all she had to indicate whether she would accept such an honour if it were offered to her. For once in her life her hand had trembled as she wrote and her reply had had to be copied out again. She kept it secret from Molly who would have found it hard not to give any kind of hint to her Fundadoran friends, and it would have been round the island in ten minutes.

When the missive finally arrived it was almost like the old Balmoral days. A thick official envelope, Molly standing by expectantly, Marjorie slitting the envelope open, looking at the contents, pausing. Molly becoming excited, Marjorie drawing herself up to her full height. 'Molly,' she said, 'I have some news.'

'Of course. What is it, Marjorie? Have you won something?'

'You might put it like that.' She paused again. 'I have been awarded the MBE.'

'MBE?'

'I have been made a Member of the Order of the British Empire!'

Molly sank into the nearest chair. 'Who by?' she gasped.

'The Queen.' Belle stood to attention. 'Good dog,' and Belle received a pat.

Marjorie explained patiently. 'Important people, like the Governor of Fundador, put forward the names of the people they think deserve an honour. Buckingham

Palace officials - very high officials - advise the Queen, and she takes their advice. They appear to have thought it justified in my case.'

'How could they know anything about you? How could they know how clever you have always been?'

'It's for what I've done *here*, Molly. My committee work. My organisation of so many things. Of course I take it as a leader, on behalf of my troops, as Father would have put it. You are entitled to feel proud of being one of my troop, Molly dear.'

'Oh, Marjorie - I see - how wonderful.'

'And now perhaps a cup of tea?'

It would be hard to say that anyone was delighted except Molly, and of course Emily and Alma, and the Amstrads when they heard. 'Mother and Father would have been so proud,' said Molly. And Marjorie agreed.

The ex-pats were very put out. None could think of a more worthy recipient from amongst their number but after all, Mrs Bryce had been there such a short time. They told each other about episodes they had witnessed where Mrs Bryce had been seen to be manoeuvring herself into positions where she could be seen by the Governor or speak quietly to his wife.

'Look how she ousted Mrs Bandera.'

'Yes, and took over completely when Mrs Ortega was ill.'

'And she forced herself on the Bridge Club.'

'Still, that's hardly a "good work".'

'No, but it got her in with us, which meant she went everywhere.'

'She certainly used us.'

On these occasions Marjorie was strictly referred to as Mrs Bryce. Had she been interested she could have judged her popularity, or usefulness, by the way the expats addressed her. If she seemed above herself, gaining solitary credit at Government House, she was Mrs Bryce. If she was engaged in something which might bring them into closer contact with Government House, it was Marjorie. Admittedly, this familiarity did not mean they liked her better, only that she could be of use to them. So far as she was concerned she preferred to be known as Mrs Bryce, which showed respect and kept them in their place.

The Fundadorans were less unkind. They saw it as the officer class being rewarded for service, not over and above the call of duty but the service expected of a good officer. And there was her interest in dogs which would surely meet with the approval of the Queen. Obviously Molly had gone native, so she had no chance. They realised how difficult it was on the island to find people in the upper strata - such as it was - who were worthy of recognition. And who, once recognised, were not in danger of being totally ostracised by the rest of Fundador. Not because they felt there were others more worthy but because it must have required a vast amount of personal effort behind the scenes, and an unpleasant desire to be singled out.

People either moved quickly away from Marjorie or rushed to congratulate her. Sometimes a member of the former group could not get away in time and was forced into comment. Mrs Venables was one such. She found herself inside the butcher's, a small establishment, with no way of escape except by passing close to Marjorie. Obliged to speak she said 'I've just heard the news.'

Marjorie took this as a form of congratulation. 'Thank you *so* much. Quite undeserved.'

Mrs Venables' muttered 'Indeed' went unnoticed as Marjorie continued. 'It would not have been possible without so many helpers ...'

Mrs Venables squeezed past and out into the street, Marjorie's voice fading yet pursuing '... such loyalty ... an honour ...' and Mrs Venables escaped up the street, grinding her teeth.

So far as the men were concerned, both ex-pat and Fundadoran, there was admiration for Marjorie mixed with acute dislike. It was the Thatcher syndrome in miniature. She was certainly a leader, and they could see that, as Marjorie had divined so clearly, the island was exactly the right size for her talents, and for her to achieve what she wanted from life.

There was one exception among the men, however, and that was Eustace Proctor. He was an ardent Royalist. He had once met the Queen Mother and she had been much taken with his old fashioned courtesy. It had been whispered that she had asked him to join her household, but no-one could believe he would not have accepted. It would have exactly suited him. No need to be involved with the sordid details of life, no shopping, no ghastly conversations about the price of houses, or the price of anything for that matter.

If the Queen was pleased to honour Mrs Bryce with the MBE then Eustace Proctor, as a loyal subject, would bow the knee. He met her down Main Street one morning, with Belle in train. 'Excuse me, Ma'am,' he said, bowing stiffly. 'I wish to offer you my deepest congratulations on the award which Her Majesty the Queen has been pleased to bestow upon you.'

Marjorie was delighted with this little speech. 'Thank you very much, Mr Proctor. It is most kind of you. I am very conscious of the honour which has been done to me.'

'Indeed Ma'am. As you know, I keep myself to myself, so I am not aware of the circumstances which have led to this award. But if it is my Sovereign's wish that you should be recognised in this way then it is also my wish.' He doffed his Panama hat and marched off, clutching to him his latest purchase of a jumbo-sized packet of Daz.

Once everyone was used to the idea of Marjorie being something of a celebrity they got on with their speculations about the hotel. No-one was surprised to learn that Marjorie was involved with it. What was she not involved with? The joke going round was 'Have you heard the latest about Mrs Bryce? She is moving into Government House and the Governor and his wife are taking over Villa Marmol!' Some people believed it. Anything was possible. She might even be the architect of the hotel. In the eyes of the Fundadorans she could be or do anything.

Local builders were not quite up to constructing an eight-storey hotel and a firm from the mainland had to be employed. This caused a great deal of trouble in the town. Up to now only the small garrison of British soldiers had competed for the local girls, and it was understood that few of them would enter into long-term relationships. However, the lads from the mainland spoke the language, and offered a glimpse of a more glamorous life. On Fundador there was one cinema, which showed not very up-to-date films. The young were perfectly happy with them until they heard of towns with at least two cinemas. Suddenly it seemed that the quality of one's life was enhanced by having a choice. Why should you have to see what Mr Rudolfo chose for you to see? It was dictatorship. Then there was the television. The Fundadorans enjoyed their local station, and nothing better than to see themselves being interviewed, and holding forth abut the chances of one local football team against the other and similar riveting events. Then there were the imported soaps - *Neighbours*, old episodes of *Dallas* and *Coronation Street* were compulsory viewing and everybody discussed the latest developments. The young preferred *Dallas*, where they felt they could identify with the glamorous characters. Who knew what opportunities would open up for them in the future? Their elders preferred *Coronation Street*, where family life was solid and people were *au fond* perfectly contented with their lot. When Molly's friends talked of *Coronation Street* she never mentioned the fact that the episodes they saw were so ancient that even she could not remember them. In fact at first she had been totally confused when she thought that she was seeing new episodes and yet everyone seemed to have regained their youth. Marjorie pointed out to her the true facts of the matter.

'I shouldn't tell your friends,' said Marjorie. 'They'll want to know what's happened in the interim and you'll never remember.'

Molly reluctantly agreed. She would get in a terrible muddle if she tried to explain all the ins and outs of the plot over the past few years. Anyway she was enjoying watching the old episodes, and perhaps when they got more up-to-date she would say something to Mavis.

But now the men from the mainland scoffed at the local television station and its old episodes of the soaps and they taunted the girls with their old fashioned way of life and the slow pace of Fundador. It appeared that on the mainland there were three television programmes to chose from. Once more it seemed that the Fundadorans were deprived. There were lots of jokes about coming out of the Stone Age and the young became very aggressive about it at home.

Fundadoran people did visit the mainland from time to time, but usually when they were adult and able to appreciate the difference in life style - when they could see their island as a wonderful refuge from the noise and dirt of the mainland towns. And if there were a particularly bright boy, Professor Alberto would tutor him for a British University. They often married English girls and returned for holidays from time to time, always maintaining they would rather live on Fundador but there were no job opportunities for people as well qualified as they had become, and this was true.

A camp was constructed at the hotel site so that the builders could stay on the island all week, and on Saturday mornings a special ferry was sent over to collect them and return them to their wives and girl friends. On Saturday mornings the Fundadoran girls lined the dockside, waving and shouting endearments, and the men arrived back home to a similar reception. It was the best time they had ever had.

It was all intolerable so far as the local men were concerned. Builders from the site who were unwise enough to visit local bars in the evenings were invariably beaten up and the Court was in session almost every day, unheard of since war time when Naval ships had called in and the crews got out of hand.

Many of the girls were kept at home after sundown and there was a lot of animosity in hitherto happy families.

Altogether it was a very disrupting time for the island and it lasted until the spring. By the time of the spring rains the hotel was structurally completed, the inside ready to be finished off and decorated. Only six Fundadoran girls suffered any serious withdrawal symptoms and two of them ran away to the mainland. But by degrees life settled down to its former pleasant jog.

Jens Amstrad had been over quite regularly to ensure that the work was finished on time, since if the roof had not been on by the time of the rains the whole project would have foundered. He was very happy with the building and it was now a matter of keeping a strict eye on the installation of baths, showers, lavatories and so on. As soon as one room was ready, part of a suite on the top floor, Jens and Astrid came to stay. The decor was all to be light and airy. Not the English home from home which Marjorie espoused at the Villa Marmol but a Danish home from home, much more in keeping with the climate.

The Amstrads were so grateful to the sisters for all they had done - Marjorie getting the bulk of the credit even though they knew that Molly had done all the leg work - that they determined that when they were not on the island Marjorie and Molly should use the suite for their visitors.

Emily and Alma could stay there, at least some of the time. Alma wrote often, on Winnie the Pooh notelets, and Emily wrote from time to time. She said Alma liked school and she liked her job, so they were both happy. The idea of two weeks at Fundador in the school holidays was wonderful but Emily could only save a very little. She hated to let them finance their trip, but that was the only way they would be able to come. There was no problem here as Molly, and even Marjorie, were quite prepared to help out. Molly said it would give them great pleasure, and to Molly's delight Emily accepted at once.

Jens and Astrid decided to have a little opening ceremony at the hotel. The first cruise ship to have any of their passengers booked into the hotel was arriving on 20th of July and Molly thought it would be exciting if Emily and Alma could come then even if Alma had to miss a couple of weeks' school. Astrid said that the week after the opening she and Jens would be going back to Denmark for a while, so after a week at the villa, Emily and Alma could stay in the suite.

Astrid was charming. Tall, slim and fair, and she was very efficient. If she had a fault it was one not unknown in Danes - an inability to judge other countries by any but her own high standards. Her voice would take on a special sadness as she looked at some particularly quaint Fundadoran workmanship, saying 'In Denmark we would never allow such a thing.' The hygiene in local food shops brought on a spate of 'In Denmark - ' comments, but more in sorrow than in any hope of bringing about changes. However her presence ensured that the Fundadoran installers of baths and basins, lavatories and showers, carried out their work well above their usual standards. They were so impressed with what they were doing that they brought their families along in the evenings to inspect progress by torch light.

There was a lot to be done to get the hotel finished in every detail by the opening date. And the inhabitants had a lot to do as well. One of the first things which had to be sorted out was whether the ex-pats would attend the opening. It was a question of whether to show Marjorie that they did not consider her that important (they had heard that she was to perform the opening ceremony), or whether to be seen there by the Governor and his wife. The latter consideration, plus a large dollop of curiosity, won the day.

Mrs Caleta was known to be the best dressmaker on the island. She only had to look at a picture of a dress in a magazine to be able to create it in any shape or size. Everyone had to use her since she was the only person who knew in advance who had chosen which model, so she was kept very busy. And the appointments at Hair Magic were a close run thing in the week before the opening. No time for the usual exchange of gossip as the ladies rushed from basin to chair to dryer.

Marjorie as usual had one of her ideas. Since everyone was so excited about the opening of the hotel, and since it was happening on a Saturday, why not have some kind of a fair on the North Shore and raise money for the RSPCA? And as usual everyone, except Marjorie, set to with a will. Unlike the fête, no committee was needed, everyone would do whatever they wanted to do and they would be trusted to hand over their proceeds - well, most of their proceeds - to the Society. Also, unlike the fête, it involved all the Fundadorans, since various items had to be constructed. There was to be a carousel, a coconut shy, a firing range, donkey rides along the sand, and lots of stalls selling local produce. The ex-pats decided that since they would be too elegantly clad to ride on a carousel or throw wooden balls at coconuts they would watch the proceedings from the hotel patio, and one or two of them would look after a stall close to the hotel, explaining the aims of the local RSPCA.

The ship arrived before lunch and the opening was to be at two o'clock. Down on the dock there were the taxi and an array of donkeys, all decked out with ribbons and rosettes. Amos had a white ribbon across the bonnet of his taxi as if for a wedding. Passengers coming ashore made for the taxi, jostling each other to get there first, but it had been booked for Emily and Alma. Molly was there to meet them and she and Amos were overjoyed to see Alma again. She had grown quite a lot, and her hair was cut short, but she still had her fringe and her open friendly face. Emily was the most changed. She had blossomed, and Molly hardly recognised her.

'It's so wonderful to see you,' said Emily, and Alma just threw herself into Molly's arms. Amos excitedly bundled them into the taxi, and tied their suitcases on the top with rope he had purloined from the scaffolding - there had been lots of loot collected from the building site when the hotel was finished. The builders were very half-hearted in clearing the site, and the Fundadorans reckoned they were doing them a good turn.

As the taxi set off for the villa the rest of the hotel guests found themselves following in the footsteps of donkeys, on which their baggage had been loaded. 'Only a small walk,' they were assured, and all but one couple decided to find it very quaint, something to write home about. The last to come ashore were a middle-aged couple who did not find it at all quaint or picturesque. They asked when the taxi would return and were told it would soon be back if they liked to wait, and they did. Standing aloof and looking steadfastly up the Main Street, waiting impatiently for Amos to return, the woman said 'I really wondered whether it was wise to stay in such a god-forsaken place. I expect the hotel will be only half built and we'll get legionnaires' disease or salmonella poisoning.'

'Come on, it won't be so bad. Just think how much we'll appreciate Bournemouth when we get home.'

Quite soon a cloud of dust announced Amos' return. Mrs Whalley, for it was she, looked at it disdainfully. Amos took out a large dirty duster and flicked it over the back seat, which had already been dusted off by his previous passengers' pretty summer dresses. He ushered the Whalleys in, as if they were royalty, and they set off on the short trip to the North Shore. Rounding the corner, Mr Whalley was relieved to see that the hotel was complete; it was painted white, with blue woodwork. There were little flags hanging over the windows and the front entrance, and their fellow passengers were laughing and talking over their luggage which had been deposited at the bottom of the steps. There were some quips at the expense of the Whalleys as they stepped out of their bridal taxi.

From the hotel came three town boys, smartened up out of all recognition, and they carried the luggage inside. At the Reception Desk, Jens' nephew, Hendrik, was dealing efficiently with the guests, and attractive Fundadoran girls, in blue dresses with white aprons, flitted about. There was one lift and this was under the control of Amos' brother, so Amos took the opportunity of carrying in one of the Whalley suitcases to wish him well. He said to Mr Whalley 'This is Antoni, my brother. He is the lift officer. He is a good man. He will not let you down - ha ha, let you down, eh?'

Mr Whalley said impatiently 'Yes, yes. How much do I owe you?' and he was pleased to note that as yet the local people had not thought of charging exorbitant prices to tourists. No doubt that would come.

Mrs Whalley had to admit that the hotel was well planned and comfortable. They had a view over the bay.

'I thought it would be good if it was Scandinavian,' said Mr Whalley smugly. 'Let's unpack and see what the rest of the place is like.'

Grudgingly Mrs Whalley agreed that, so far, it seemed clean and well run.

There was a free selection of *smørrebrød* laid out in the dining room, accompanied by Danish lager. Jens had imported a minor chef from Denmark who, with his wife, had one of the staff rooms at the back of the hotel. The dining room was festooned with paper decorations and, probably for the only time in its existence, the hotel was full of utterly contented people. The guests were relieved that everything was exactly as suggested in the brochure, and the staff were relieved that all they had been told to do seemed to be right.

At Villa Marmol things had settled down to normal. Matty had greeted Alma like a long lost friend and in the kitchen her shouts of happiness and welcome continued throughout lunch.

Alma said to Marjorie 'You haven't changed at all Aunt Marjorie. You're just the same.'

'So I should hope. Why should I change?'

'Well, the medal. I mean, getting a medal from the Queen must make you feel different. Imagine the Queen knowing *you*!'

'Of course the Queen doesn't know me,' she said. 'People who do special things have their names put forward, and then she agrees to their being honoured in this way.' Marjorie patted her hair and pushed in a hair pin which had been straying.

'What did you do?' asked Alma excitedly. 'Did you save a life?'

'No, I just did my duty. I did what I saw to be my duty to my fellow human beings.'

'Yes but - '

'Now, Alma, that's enough. Your Aunt Marjorie helped people to help themselves, and that's a very great thing to be able to do.'

Alma was quiet. She wondered why it was better to tell people what to do than to do it. She looked at Aunt Molly. Surely she should have a medal too? But Molly was beaming at her sister and obviously felt very proud of her.

Alma had to ask just one more question. 'Aunt Marjorie, when you've got your medal will you wear it on a chain round your neck?'

'No, that would not be appropriate, Alma. Now hurry up or we'll be late for the opening.'

By ten to two most of the guests were on the patio and most of the townspeople were by the side of the steps and in the road. The Whalleys looked around them. The bell boys were handing out cards which had on them in gold writing 'Welcome to Fundador, welcome to the Hotel Amstrad. Opening ceremony to be performed by Mrs Bryce MBE.' The name meant nothing to the Whalleys.

'Some local big-wig, I suppose. It's all a bit pathetic,' said Mrs Whalley.

Her husband interrupted her. 'Look over there, by the rostrum - '

'Rostrum? You mean that upturned box?'

'Yes, yes. That girl. I'm sure I've seen her before.'

'On the boat, I think, with her mother.'

'I keep thinking it has something to do with Bournemouth. Wasn't she the girl who went to one of the weddings? You know - next door - '

'Oh *yes*. What on earth can she be doing here? Those poor dears. They had their little fling, didn't they.'

Mr Whalley grabbed her arm again. 'Do stop grabbing at me,' said Mrs Whalley impatiently. 'What is it now?'

'That plump woman a bit further on. Isn't she - ?'

'Good heavens, it's the one who walked behind.'

'I never saw her on board.'

'If she's staying at the hotel let's make sure she doesn't try to get into conversation. She'll never remember us. After all, we never actually spoke.'

'Can't think how we never spotted her on board - oh, here we go.'

'Rather a posh car. They don't allow people to bring cars on to the island so it must be the Governor.'

The Governor and his wife got out and a few people clapped. They smiled and Jens Amstrad, who had been waiting for them, led them to their seats behind the 'rostrum'.

Mrs Whalley approved of them. He in his naval uniform and she in a cool pink dress, and wearing a charming matching straw hat. Probably bio-degradable straw, thought Mrs Whalley, who had only just heard of this phenomenon. She felt that there must be someone on the island as sophisticated as she was, and she determined it must be the Governor's wife.

'I'm surprised they bother,' she said to her husband. He was still looking perplexedly at Molly.

The crowd murmured as they saw Amos' taxi coming back into view, coughing and spluttering as a result of so much activity.

'That dreadful taxi,' said Mrs Whalley.

Union Jack in front, balloons behind, and still the white ribbons.

'How absurd.'

It drew up at the steps and Jens went forward to open the door and help Marjorie out. All the ex-pats were wearing hats, as they did for church and the Garden party, and as Marjorie knew they would wear large ones she wore a small one. One in fact composed entirely of different petals. Her wedding hat.

Mr Whalley suddenly again gripped his wife's arm. Mrs Whalley turned on him. 'If you do that once again I'll - '

Mr Whalley almost shouted 'It's HRH. It bloody well *is* HRH!'

Everyone looked at Mr Whalley in astonishment. 'Which one? Who is she?' came from all sides. Mrs Whalley was appalled. Firstly by the vision of Marjorie grandly ascending the steps of the hotel on the arm of the manager, secondly by the disgrace of having her husband shout out 'bloody', and last but far from least by the Governor's wife looking coldly in their direction.

Marjorie made a short speech. She welcomed everyone to the Hotel and she thanked the Governor and his wife for coming along. It had been felt that to break a bottle of champagne might be dangerous - and on what? So Jens had been carefully easing out the cork from a champagne bottle and at the crucial moment he handed it to Marjorie. She just had time to say 'I declare the Hotel Amstrad open' when the cork shot into the air. The townspeople cheered, and those in its path raised their hands, competing to catch it. Marjorie retained her dignity as the champagne bubbled over her hand. Jens took the bottle and one of the little maids ran forward and dried Marjorie's hand with a large linen table napkin. Marjorie inclined her head in thanks, the girl blushed at being suddenly in the limelight, and the local newspaper photographer pressed the button. Champagne was served on the patio and the townspeople now rushed towards the fair.

The Whalleys retired to their room and for a while Mrs Whalley was lost for the appropriate words. They lay on their beds, Mr Whalley reading a Dick Francis paperback, Mrs Whalley pretending to read *Vogue*.

'Well,' she said finally, 'she certainly chose a very small pool in which to be a very average sized fish.'

'Right,' said Mr Whalley, turning a page.

'How the Governor and his wife survive in such a sterile atmosphere I can't imagine. I suppose they're used to having to mix with inferior minds.' She paused. 'I mean, two weeks here is all I could take.' A sour note had been struck and she would be glad to regain a foothold in a society which she understood, one in which she and her husband knew they were superior to most people and inferior to none. The cruise ship would be back in a fortnight and all that the Whalleys needed from life could be found on board.

Tea was served on the patio at four o'clock and Marjorie suggested that Molly should go and find Emily and Alma and bring them back for tea. Molly had strained her back the day before, lifting a heavy patient in hospital, and was limping slightly.

Jens was concerned. 'I should go. The poor lady is lumping.'

'Limping, actually,' said Marjorie. 'No, she likes to be busy. She'll forget about it and it will get better in no time.'

The Whalleys asked for tea in their room.

Alma brought Tessie back with her. They had been a little wary of each other at the fair, doing things separately, until they shared a horse on the carousel. This brought them into giggling companionship once more and they found that they had both grown up - at least that is how they saw it. It meant that they didn't wish to scrabble on the ground for bits and pieces, as they had at the fête, and they were very happy to take their turns at the coconut shy, and for a ride on a donkey. They helped the small children onto the backs of the donkeys, and if they were very small they rode with them. Emily, liking Tessie, couldn't understand why Aunt Marjorie had apparently said she was a 'bad influence'. She asked Colonel Amstrad if Tessie might come for tea and he was happy to see that Alma had a friend on the island already. He and his wife thought Alma was a charming child and liked to think of Marjorie and Molly having such a young friend, who would see them into their old age.

In their beds that night at the Villa Marmol it took a little while for everyone to get settled. Alma had her old room and, kneeling by the window, she was enchanted to see that everything was the same. Matty's friend climbed the stairs to her room as usual, the Pardoe kitchen issued forth the familiar aroma of spices, the trees were etched against the sky, and there was the mixed scent of flowers and sea air. Once in bed she fell asleep to the sound of the surf breaking gently on the shore.

Molly finally found a position comfortable to her back and thought for a moment about the day. It had all gone well, as of course it would if Marjorie had anything to do with it. She had felt very proud of her sister when she opened the hotel. Really she was someone on the island. Molly had overheard a comment about Marjorie which had thrilled her: 'She must have royal blood'. Well, that was perhaps going too far, but she knew what they meant. Of course she didn't know that the speaker had heard Mr Whalley call Marjorie HRH, and she herself hadn't heard him. She drifted off into a contented sleep.

Marjorie was equally satisfied. At the back of her mind she was a little sad to think that there was no further peak for her to scale. She felt that she could now give up the committees - perhaps she could become President of all of them, and appear once a year with a few words of congratulation and encouragement. She would see. *The Game of Life* ... had little more to offer. She moved it to the bottom drawer of her dressing table. It was there just in case, but she doubted whether she would need it again. She creamed her face and pinned up her hair, carefully removed the bedspread and equally carefully got into bed. Nothing kept her awake, no worries and no future plans. She lay back and was soon asleep.

Emily had the small back room and she found it very pleasant. She had a novel but she preferred to lie in the dark and think. She was amazed to see how the sisters had fitted into Fundadoran society. At first she was rather shocked that Marjorie was so much the General - she thought of that without knowing the views of the Fundadoran ladies in the patio of the Club, who had transferred their sobriquet to Marjorie.

What did Marjorie really do? She spent a good deal of time with her feet up as far as Emily could gather. Today she said she had very much missed her siesta and Molly, concerned, had confirmed that this was a daily habit. She went out on monthly forays as Chairman of various committees, told everyone what to do, and returned to put her feet up, no doubt, whilst Molly ran to get her cool drinks or sustenance. She treated Molly like a slave. Emily supposed she always had, and it was obvious that Molly did not mind. So why should Emily mind? She fell into a fitful sleep, sure she could still feel the movement of the ship.

A few days in the villa only served to strengthen Emily's feelings. She saw that Marjorie was incredibly selfish, yet she realised that she did no harm, and although she kept Molly on the run when she was at home surely Molly could have rebelled long ago? She was obviously fulfilled.

It seemed unfair, somehow, that Molly should do so much and get so little recognition and Marjorie do so little and receive such wide acclaim, but there was no point in unsettling things, and Emily tried to save Molly's steps whenever she could.

But it didn't stop Emily spending a great deal of time over the next few days pondering on their characters. She compared them with other people she had known over the years and she had to admit that it never worked to act out of character. If Marjorie had met them at the dock and run forward to hug Alma, Alma would have been alarmed. If she appeared in the hospital and insisted on washing someone's feet or writing a letter for them, they would have been embarrassed. Her image would be shattered. No-one would say 'What a pleasant change has come over Mrs Bryce.' No, they would shake their heads and say 'Poor Mrs Bryce, she's not the woman she was.' And should Molly suddenly start to boss people about, or look down her nose in that certain way which Marjorie did when anyone dared to disagree with her, she would be thoroughly disapproved of. No, to act out of character was a dangerous thing, and something which neither of them would be tempted to do.

Yet Marjorie knew that a small gesture on her part, a kind word here and there from time to time - say twice a year - if sufficiently unexpected and public, was important. It meant that should the odd, unappreciative person say to a group of friends, in a moment of irritation, 'Really, Mrs Bryce is too bad. She bosses everyone around and she lets her sister do everything whilst she spends half her time with her feet up', another would say 'Ah, but she has a heart of gold. You should have seen her the other day with Mrs Haselhurst's dog, when she thought it had something in its paw. She was on her knees - ' 'Really? On her *knees*?' - 'Yes, and when Mrs Bandera was in hospital she took her a bunch of grapes.'

'I suppose it's a front. She has to hide her feelings. She's had a sad life you know.'

'They say she was devoted to her husband and nursed him through a long illness - she has hinted at many hours spent beside a sick bed.'

'I think, for her, it is torture even to enter a hospital.'

And so on.

'Mrs Jessop, of course, is a simple soul. She finds it easy - she doesn't feel so deeply.'

'And what would she do if she wasn't on the go?'

It was this imaginary but very likely conversation which Emily did resent. Marjorie must be aware of how she manipulated people. But so must the people she manipulated, in their hearts. It was as if Marjorie was a consummate actress and her public admired the way she played her part. Even perhaps obtained some vicarious satisfaction in helping her to succeed.

And Marjorie would continue to take it easy, and Molly would wear herself out to her heart's content.

Moving to the hotel, Emily and Alma entered into a new relationship. As a Barnardo's girl Emily had had a happy childhood but she never thought of adults as people who might be friends. They were administrators, advisers and sometimes figures of authority. Never companions. There were cuddles for the very young, but they were all encouraged to grow up as soon as possible. Emily therefore found it easy and natural to be affectionate towards Alma when she was small but later she treated her as she herself had been treated at Barnardo's, as a small adult. This made Alma very independent and rather old for her age.

Now Emily found they could be friends. With Molly so busy and Marjorie occupied with her own unspecified activities during the day, they only went up to the villa in the late afternoon. During the day they swam, or walked or played table tennis - and talked.

One day Alma said suddenly: 'Is it better to tell people what to do or to do things?'

'Well, it can be all right to influence people, if it's for good.'

'What's influence?'

'Having people do what you want them to do. Not always telling them. Sometimes by example.'

'But that would mean doing things yourself. I mean just telling - '

Emily smiled. 'You're thinking of the aunts?'

'Yes.'

'I've thought about them a lot too. I don't think people decide, just like that. I think part of it is their character and part of it is how other people treat them.'

'So you might be born to be nice and then, if your parents were horrid to you, you would end up horrid.'

Emily thought, not for the first time, that Alma was an amazingly understanding little girl. And it was then that she realised that she was in fact a very understanding person and that to keep thinking of her only as a child was absurd.

Alma went on: 'Tessie told me she used to be naughty because her father didn't like her. And now she's good because the nuns do like her. I don't know what her mother thinks - she's too busy with the boys.'

'Is it a big family?'

'Tessie has twin brothers - about three or four years old I think. Actually - ' this was a new word she had picked up from Hendrik Amstrad. He was often heard at Reception saying 'Actually the rooms are all air conditioned,' or 'Actually lunch will be served at one o'clock.'

'Actually,' said Alma 'one of the twins is always laughing and the other is always crying. That must be just their characters because they both get treated the same.'

'I suppose if no-one is kind or unkind, if life just goes on an even keel - '

'Keel like in a boat?'

'Yes. Well, then you end up with most of what you were born with. I think that's probably what happened with the aunts. From what Molly says they were very happy at home. They just developed naturally. Not much outside influence. I remember you said last year, one being smiley and the other serious it keeps things just right - '

'On an even keel!'

'That's it.'

'If they were both like Aunt Molly nothing would ever get done. They wouldn't be here, and here is where they like to be.' Alma thought for a while. 'You influence me don't you?'

'Only now, while you're young. Later on you'll be able to do what you like. I know you'll be very wise. Wiser than me I expect.'

'Well I'm in charge now - we're going to swim!'

'Right.' And they went off laughing, to change.

Two days before the ship returned there was the Government House Garden Party. Emily had been taken by Marjorie to sign 'The Book' the day after she arrived, and the Whalleys were the only other passengers who knew it was the thing to do. They hoped it would mean an invitation to Government House, and in fact it was perfectly timed for the Garden Party.

Everyone dressed up for the occasion and the ladies wore their special hats, slightly changed from the year before by the addition or subtraction of a bow or flower. The men wore smart summer suiting and, apart from Eustace Proctor, no hats. Eustace wore his yellowing Panama.

Marjorie introduced Emily to the Governor and his wife and the latter asked after Alma. 'I met her last year, at the fête. A dear girl. She wrote a poem.'

'She's out with a friend she met last year,' said Emily.

'How nice for her - oh, excuse me,' she turned to a couple who had sidled up. 'I don't think we've met?'

'Jack Whalley, from Bournemouth. My wife - '

'How d' you do.'

'How d' you do.' They shook hands.

The Governor's wife, with a social memory, said quickly, 'Oh, you must meet Mrs Bryce and Mrs Jessop. They came from Bournemouth.'

Molly smiled and was prepared to talk, but Marjorie said repressively, 'We lived there once - for a while. It was not a place I could enjoy.'

'Balmoral!' said Mrs Whalley, rather too loudly.

'No, Bournemouth,' replied Marjorie haughtily. Molly gulped and Marjorie said 'Molly, I don't think you know Mr Proctor,' and propelled her across the lawn.

'Why didn't you talk to them?' asked Molly, confused. 'They must have lived near to us.'

'They lived next door or I'm a Dutchman.'

Molly stared at her. She opened her mouth and Marjorie intercepted her next remark - 'and don't repeat Dutchman. It's just an expression. We ignored them then and we will ignore them now.'

'If you say so,' said Molly uncertainly.

'Mr Proctor, you haven't met my sister have you? Mrs Jessop.'

'My dear lady, I fear I live a quiet life. I meet few people.' He paused and surveyed Molly. 'You must visit me - perhaps you would like to come to church one Sunday?'

Marjorie was surprised by this invitation to Molly. Mr Proctor, who was known to be very alarmed by 'the ladies', only ever entertained known oddities. Was Molly really such an oddity?

Molly immediately agreed. As a family they had never attended church. It was rather as if no-one had ever suggested going for a walk. She had only taken walks when one of her parents had suggested it, and she had enjoyed it. Now she would enjoy church. In her naive way she said 'Can I come next Sunday?' Mr Proctor raised his Panama hat and she took this to be a gesture of assent.

Mrs Whalley was busy being grand with the Governor and his wife and she allowed Marjorie's rebuff to rest in the back of her mind until they got back to their hotel room. 'Really, that woman. Bournemouth "not a place I could enjoy",' and she did a rather poor imitation of Marjorie looking down her nose. 'What *did* she mean? She was no-one in Bournemouth.'

'That's what she meant I expect,' said Mr Whalley.

'It was the way she said it which most annoyed me. As if Bournemouth was the back of beyond. The

Governor's wife smiled as if she agreed, but of course she has to be agreeable to everyone. It's part of the job. No-one in their right mind could pretend Fundador is anything but a total backwater. Thank God we're leaving on Friday.'

'I've enjoyed it,' said Jack Whalley.

'Oh it's all right for a visit. But that bloody woman acts as if she were the Queen of Fundador!'

'Sounds like Gilbert and Sullivan.'

'It *is* Gilbert and Sullivan - but they don't know it. That's what's so exasperating.'

They only saw Marjorie once more after that, on the Friday morning. She was walking down the Main Street with Belle. She looked neither to right nor left, so did not appear to see the Whalleys. She never acknowledged tourists anyway.

Mr Whalley said with amusement, 'Look, now the dog walks two paces behind!'

Mrs Whalley tossed her head and looked the other way. They were leaving that afternoon and as soon as they were on that boat they would be back in civilisation.

It was all go on the dockside; luggage piled high and everyone carrying extra baskets and packages. Molly had come to see Emily and Alma off. It wasn't a sad parting this time as she was sure they would come back one day. And somehow the fact that Emily and Alma were so happy together made Molly happy. Even as she hugged them, and waved them off, she was thinking of her new adventure - going to church on Sunday. She was leading a life of her own. She would not need Marjorie as much as in the past, and Marjorie would have no trouble filling her days. She groomed herself and now she took over from Matty the grooming of Belle. Belle was so intelligent. Whereas Molly would be perplexed and ask questions, Belle just listened, cocking her head on one side, totally in agreement with all that Marjorie said. Sometimes she seemed to nod, rather as Marjorie did when emphasising a point.

In their cabin the Whalleys unpacked.

'I shall be glad never to see those two again,' said Mrs Whalley. 'Really, who do they think they are? They're nobodies, that's who they are.'

'Then why do they upset you - why go on about them? We won't ever see them again.'

Mrs Whalley said 'We certainly won't' vehemently, slamming shut her empty suitcase.

'They always did live in a world of make believe,' said Mr Whalley, settling on to his bunk with his paperback.

Two decks above them, Emily and Alma leaned against the rail watching Fundador recede, until it was a speck on the horizon.

'You know what?' said Alma. 'I believe Aunt Marjorie invented it - '

'I believe she did.'

'So I think she deserved her medal.'

Emily gave her a hug.

Ten

Molly arrived at the church late for the service the following Sunday. Marjorie had tried to discourage her. 'You know what a poor singing voice you have - father always said you could never sing in tune.'

'Well I don't need to sing. I'll just mouth the words.'

'It never looks natural I'm afraid. Remember those services we watched on television at home? People opening and shutting their mouths - all out of synch.' Marjorie was rather proud of using such a technical expression. Realising Molly would have no idea what she meant she added, 'Poor timing.'

'But Harry Secombe was so wonderful - you said so yourself Marjorie.'

'There won't be anyone like that here to distract attention,' Marjorie pointed out.

Molly could not deny it. 'I'll just sit at the back then.'

Not having succeeded in dissuading her, Marjorie now achieved some satisfaction by causing a little panic.

'You're not going in those shoes, are you? It's quite a long way and the path is far from even. And you'd better take a sunshade. Have you got your glasses? The tinted ones?'

By the time Molly set off she was hot and flustered, and when she reached the church there was no-one in sight and thin, uncertain voices raised in thanks to the Lord told her that the service had started. Luckily the heat made it impractical to shut the doors so she was able to slip in and take a seat at the back of the church.

She was aware that the ex-pats attended the Chapel by Government House - it was important to be seen there - and the locals went to the Catholic church, so she was not surprised at the sparseness of the congregation here. Gazing at their backs she thought she recognised a few elderly misfits from the ex-pat and the local communities, and in the front pew Mr Proctor sat alone. He appeared to be singing one line ahead, or perhaps behind, everyone else, but the wheezing of the small portable organ, played by the little old woman who ran what she called an antique shop by the harbour, created a general effect of harmony. Even Molly was able to have a stab at *God our help in ages past*.

At the end of the service Mr Proctor marched out first, head in air, and Molly had to run after him as he strode down the dusty path.

'Mr Proctor - I - I've come,' she panted.

He stopped abruptly and she cannoned into him.

'Oh, I'm dreadfully sorry - '

'My dear lady, no harm done. "When two or three are joined together um - ah - let no man put asunder",' he ended, confusingly.

'Yes indeed,' said Molly, smiling shyly.

Mr Proctor pointed with his walking stick towards a small house, slightly apart from those leading to Main Street. 'A cup of coffee, Ma'am?'

'How kind,' and Molly followed him up the steps which led to a small veranda. He gestured towards a dilapidated deck-chair.

'Take a seat, Mrs - er - ' he said vaguely, 'and I will organise the coffee.'

'Do let me help,' said Molly, following him through the front door.

'Very good of you - mind the rugs - this way,' and Molly stepped carefully over the rugs, several on top of one another, all sizes. She also manoeuvred the pile of old *Country Life* magazines, the row of boots, a pile of newspapers, empty egg boxes and charity collecting tins, and followed Mr Proctor down the un-carpeted stairs to the kitchen.

The kitchen table was covered with old newspapers - flimsy air mail editions of *The Times* - on top of which were a selection of enormous tins. These contained Ovaltine, instant coffee, biscuits, sugar and tea. Cups and saucers and tea spoons lay about. Three eggs sat in an open egg box on the draining board, and evidence of a good English breakfast lay in the sink.

Molly's experienced eye located a tray and she rinsed two cups and saucers and a tea spoon. Mr Proctor lit the gas under an outsize black kettle.

'Thank you, Ma'am. Very civil - ' and he took the tea spoon from Molly. Opening the instant coffee tin he first attacked the rock hard contents with a long screwdriver, evidently kept on the kitchen table for this purpose. Having managed to create two pieces of a suitable size he balanced them one at a time on the teaspoon and placed one in each cup. He was careful to secure the lid of the coffee tin tightly. 'Wouldn't want it to get stale' - and he gave the lid a final tap all round with the wrong end of the screwdriver.

Molly was far from surprised or put out by any of this. She saw at once that here was a pensioner who had slipped through their net. She would say nothing for the moment but in a week or so she would arrange for a notice of the next meeting of the Retired Persons' Club to be sent to him.

Boiling water was duly poured on the coffee and, the milk looking a little doubtful, Molly said she always drank hers black. Evidently Mr Proctor did too, and taking the tray from her he ushered her upstairs. She glanced in the front room, which seemed to be so full of large pieces of furniture it would hardly be possible to get into it, let alone sit on one of the enormous armchairs, and she just had time to look over her shoulder into what must be the study. An equally full room but with a well trodden pathway to a huge oak desk. She was particularly struck by the pile of papers and envelopes on the desk, in the nearby wastepaper basket and on the floor around both. She did hope that Mr Proctor paid his bills regularly.

'Take a seat Ma'am. Please do,' and Mr Proctor placed the tray carefully on the veranda floor, and with a bow handed a cup of the ancient brew to Molly.

'Very refreshing,' she said, sipping carefully, and a rather embarrassed silence fell upon them.

Molly looked around for a subject of conversation and her eyes noted a large old fashioned container. Hoping she was right she said 'I see you have binoculars?' This was exactly the right thing to say and with relief Mr Proctor launched into a long explanation of his bird-watching activities.

Molly, her head a little on one side like a small bird herself, listened enraptured. Mr Proctor, running out of steam, paused. 'I'll lend you a book' he said, and went indoors to get one. There was some banging about as he climbed over chairs and possibly tables in the front room, but he returned in triumph, holding aloft a small battered book.

'I am sure you will enjoy this. It particularly details the birds in this part of the world and those which fly over during their migration periods. A beautiful sight - beautiful. Straight over Fundador and Assandra. Makes it all worthwhile.'

'I'm sure it does. Thank you so much,' said Molly. 'And my sister will take a great interest.'

Back at the villa, however, she aroused no enthusiasm in Marjorie.

'But Marjorie, they fly directly over here and Assandra on their way South. Mr Proctor watches them every year.'

'A very trivial occupation, bird-watching,' said Marjorie. 'Like photography. You can see all you want in magazines. Let the professionals do it. In *The Lady* last week there was a photograph of Canadian geese. That's good enough for me. But if you want to bird watch far be it for me to stand in your way.'

'No, I don't,' said Molly quickly. 'But it is interesting. So many different birds, Mr Proctor said.'

'Yes dear. I'm sure he knows a lot about them. He obviously has time on his hands. Now let's get on with the practical side of life. You haven't laid the table yet, have you?'

And off went Molly on this vital errand.

Taking a walk with Belle up to the Animal Shelter, Marjorie was pleasantly surprised to see two men sitting in earnest conversation on the bench in the Pets' Graveyard. On her approach they rose to their feet and the dark fat man said 'Good afternoon. Mrs Bryce is it not? It is to you we are indebted for this well placed bench. I am Mr Tonado, of the House of Representatives of Fundador.'

Remembering that Jens Amstrad had told her that Mr Tonado had helped him over planning permission for the hotel she said 'I am glad to meet a member of that distinguished body,' though in fact she did not hold the Representatives in high esteem, regarding them as jumped up local Councillors.

'May we vacate this seat for you, dear lady? I was myself just leaving - '

'I also,' muttered the small fair man beside him.

The trainee from Denmark at the hotel surely, thought Marjorie, and as she watched them making their way down the path towards the town she thought how splendid it was that her bench should bring people together. Two men, escaping from their hot stuffy offices, making a chance encounter, and perhaps a friendship. She sighed and looked at Belle. 'Well there you are. A wonderful view from the graves, a wonderful view for the living. I've reserved the best plot for you Belle. You'll be here one day so it's right you should get to know the place,' and she sighed again at the thought of Belle dying before her. Of course you never knew and Marjorie sat back and allowed herself a little reverie. She imagined herself in the graveyard in the town and Belle sitting, inconsolable, by her grave. People passing and shaking their heads. 'That dog adored her. But a dog cannot understand. Life must go on. The dog has not eaten or slept for seven days and nights - ' crossing themselves and passing on.

Pulling herself together Marjorie looked down at Belle, who was watching her attentively. 'You are a very intelligent dog,' she said. 'Come along, let's go home. I expect Molly will be waiting for us.'

Marjorie had no sooner told Molly of her meeting at the cemetery, and of how delighted she was to be the cause of people enjoying the beauty of the spot she had so wisely chosen when, to her surprise, Mr Tonado appeared at the front door.

'Mr Tonado, I thought you would have returned to your office. Did you leave something up at the cemetery? I'm afraid I didn't notice anything.'

'No, no, Mrs Bryce. I merely diverted myself so as to say to you - to explain to you - in case you wondered why I - we - were at the cemetery at such a time - '

'Mr Tonado I was extremely pleased. To see two busy men taking time off to sit on the bench which I had arranged at that beautiful spot, and to think you would not have had this relaxation if it were not for me - '

'Of course. And there I found that nice man from the hotel and we had a most interesting talk about hotel management, a subject of great pleasure to me. Thanks to you I made a friend and learned these things.'

'Would you like a cup of tea, Mr Tonado?'

'How very kind. Yes indeed,' and he allowed himself to be led into the drawing room where he sat in a large armchair and surveyed the room in some astonishment. To have so many things in a room, all so heavy and dark - he could not understand it. However, he wanted to keep on the right side of Marjorie and he set his heavy features in what he felt to be an appreciative expression.

Marjorie sat on the sofa whilst Molly went to see about tea. It occurred to Marjorie that, feeble as the

House of Representatives was, it might be useful to have them on her side. They had passed the plans for the Shelter without a murmur, because there was no money involved, but one day she might need money. So she smiled at Mr Tonado and gushed 'I'm glad you feel strongly about animals. Not everyone on this island feels as you do, but they are learning. And of course birds are important too.'

Molly returned with the tea and put the tray on the table in front of Marjorie. To her amazement she heard Molly saying 'As you will know, we are on the route of migrating birds - a wonderful thing - and more could be made of it.' On sudden inspiration she added 'We should have an observation post for bird-watchers!'

Mr Tonado tried to look enthusiastic but he found it very difficult. He hated pets, and he liked to trap and eat birds of all kinds. However he said heartily 'Why not? You must make a plan Mrs Bryce and put it to the House of Representatives.'

'Why not on Assandra?' continued Marjorie.

Molly chirruped with excitement, but Mr Tonado's face had inexplicably darkened. 'An observation post - on Assandra?'

'Yes, on Assandra. It is right in the path of the migrating birds. Think of the effect on tourism. There could even be some chalets - but I realise I go too fast. Let us start with the observation post.'

'Oh Marjorie, what a splendid idea. It would be wonderful,' said Molly. 'How do you get these ideas?'

'How indeed?' muttered Mr Tonado. Then 'No. No. It would not do. Quite wrong.' He paused. 'Think of those poor natives. Assandra is a memorial to a brave and wonderful people. The House of Representatives would not agree to it. In bad weather people could be stranded there. It would be disastrous.' The words came pouring out. Seeing the look of shock on the faces of the sisters he realised he had been too harsh. 'You are very kind to think of our tourist trade. I know my colleagues will be appreciative. But they will never agree. Those poor Assandrians. But - why not a post on Fundador? This would be far more appropriate. Why not on the Eastern Promontory?'

Marjorie was put out by his sudden change of tone and became stubborn. She insisted that Assandra was exactly the right place and that the post itself would be the memorial to the Assandrians.

Mr Tonado got to his feet. 'I thank you ladies for your hospitality. The tea was excellent but - yes, the Eastern Promontory - ' and he left with what Marjorie considered indecent haste.

'Oh Marjorie, it's a wonderful idea. But if they are upset over Assandra why not agree to the Eastern Promontory? It would be much easier and just as good I'm sure.' She was concerned to think of Mr Proctor having to go all the way to Assandra to enjoy this facility.

'I think Mr Tonado was very rude,' said Marjorie firmly. 'I suspect it was just because it was my idea and he wants to make it his own. Some people are funny like that. I'll speak to the Governor about it. I'm sure he'll see my point.'

'It isn't up to him, is it? I mean, the House of Representatives - '

'No, but he knows everyone. I'm sure he'll have a word in the right quarter.'

A couple of days later Marjorie was invited into the Governor's office and over a cup of coffee she explained to him her new idea.

'You certainly are full of ideas, Mrs Bryce. Quite honestly I think it may be a good one, though I rather agree that a post on the island would be simpler.'

'Yes but on Assandra they might build a few chalets so that bird-watchers could stay for a while. They would feel rather adventurous,' Marjorie added.

'How did you come to be talking to Mr Tonado about it? It's not his line of country at all.'

'I met him up at the Pets' Cemetery - he was there with one of the people from the hotel. A Dane - I think he's training for the hotel business. I was so delighted to think that people would go up there during the day, making friends - enjoying the view.'

The Governor looked dubious. 'Leave it to me, Mrs Bryce. I'll have a word with a couple of the Representatives - environment and tourism, that's the ticket. I'll keep you informed.'

The following day the Governor had a meeting with Mr Enrico whose interest was the environment, and Mr Branco, who took responsibility for tourism.

Mr Branco was impressed. 'She certainly has ideas, and one can say that she has taken Fundador to her heart.'

'Most certainly she has,' agreed Mr Enrico.

'To my mind such a project should be carried out on Fundador - you might have problems being responsible for people who were thirty miles away. But what I cannot understand is why Mr Tonado should be so concerned about it,' said the Governor.

'You are right,' agreed Mr Branco. 'Did you know he is trying to get a Bill drafted to forbid any activity ever on Assandra?'

'Yes,' said Mr Enrico, 'and he says it must remain as a memorial to the worthy Assandrians!'

The Governor broke in: 'If I may say so, no-one on Fundador gave a toss for the Assandrians before they died, and I don't think anyone really ever thinks of them now.'

'You have reason. We did not worry our heads about them. But we did not need to until they became ill.' Mr Enrico's face expressed regret, but he raised his arms and dropped them expressively.

'Seriously, Your Excellency, we do feel concern over Mr Tonado's attitude. Does he know of some activity already going on over there do you suppose?' said Mr Branco.

'Drugs or something?' the Governor suggested.

Mr Enrico said: 'That is what we wondered. You will remember a little difficulty we had two years ago?'

'The drug smuggling affair?'

'Yes. Mr Tonado was implicated but he managed to extricate himself. We always felt he was involved, nevertheless.'

'Tourism depends on the island being - what do you call it - an oasis?' Mr Branco looked worried.

The Governor agreed that Fundador had always been an oasis of peace and tranquillity, and this is what would make the hotel such a success, and such a boon to the tourist trade; and if it also had the reputation for birdwatching this would be just the right touch. But any suspicion of drugs in the area could ruin their plans.

'Would you like me to send someone over from the garrison to have a look around?'

The Representatives looked relieved. That was exactly what they would like, and it was decided that a boat full of troops would go to Assandra the following evening, after dark. All agreed that the operation must be kept absolutely secret. If there was nothing, well and good, though it might be wise to make it a regular operation.

'You'll tell your Chief Minister what our plans are? We'll need his consent.'

'We will.'

The troops were delighted to have something to do and as soon as it was dark enough for them to set off they clambered aboard. Luckily the sea was not too rough as one or two of them were bad sailors.

'I've been sick in Poole Harbour,' boasted Private Hollings.

'You try that on tonight, my lad, and you'll be overboard with a rope round your middle,' said Corporal Duckworth. 'Not too good being towed for thirty miles.'

'You ever tried it, Corp?'

'None of your cheek now. Everything ready? All aboard? OK, we're off.'

Corporal Duckworth reckoned a sing-song would be in order and once they were out of earshot of Fundador there was much singing and a good deal of bawdy conversation which helped to pass the time. On seeing Assandra ahead, a dark and rather sinister outline against the night sky, they became quiet. They were armed but had orders not to shoot except in self defence, and to be truthful they did not expect to find anyone to shoot at. They soon ascertained that the bay was uninhabited, as they had thought it would be, and Corporal Duckworth said 'We'll just go round the back, then it's sandwiches, coffee and back to Fundador.'

To their surprise, on rounding the corner they could vaguely see some long low buildings. 'Pre-fabs,' whispered Corporal Duckworth. 'What the hell can it be?'

A landing stage had been built and they had no trouble tying up to it and climbing the metal steps. Moving as quietly as they could they approached the first building. At the back of it was a light, and they could smell fish frying. 'Cor, wouldn't mind some of that,' one of them whispered. Corporal Duckworth led the way. Gun at the ready he kicked open the door. A square, middle-aged man confronted him. He was in fisherman's gear, and for a moment the Corporal thought he must be a fisherman who'd drifted onto the island and found these huts. But who had put the huts there?

The man waved a fork in the air and said 'Nex week you say. Nex week!'

'What's next week?' asked Corporal Duckworth, roughly grabbing the man by the shoulder. 'What're you talking about?'

With difficulty the man explained that he was a watchman. People were coming next week. He didn't know what for. They had hired him on the mainland and he wanted to go home. 'For the money,' he kept saying.

Leaving a couple of soldiers with him the rest of them searched the buildings but found nobody else. There was some kind of laboratory, computers, a couple of offices, a small kitchen and a dormitory. Attached to the back of the laboratory was a large cage.

Corporal Duckworth glanced at the files, then with growing interest started to read them. Following him into the office Lance Corporal Watkins asked 'Found anything?'

'Well, it looks as if they're going to carry out experiments. Look at all these memos - marked SECRET - there's some funny business going on. Here, you're a quick reader, see if you can work it out.'

An hour later they felt they knew all they needed to know. It was a laboratory for experiments on animals. It had to do with research into a cure for Alzheimer's Disease, and it seemed to be essential that the experiments were carried out on live animals.

'Swine,' muttered 'Soppy' Martin.

'Once they got this going they'd get into worse things,' Duckworth said, knowingly.

'What sort of things?' asked Watkins.

'Haven't a clue, but I don't watch television for nothing, my son. Come on, let's see if the phone works.'

To Duckworth's amazement it did, and he rang HQ with the news. It was agreed that another boat would come to take off the watchman and the files, and bring in supplies so that the rest of them could wait on the island until the owners of the laboratory turned up. It would have to be the following night, since if anyone on Fundador was involved they must not have any idea of what was happening.

Corporal Duckworth's men were delighted with the whole affair. It seemed unlikely that there would be bloodshed since the people - scientists or whatever - would not be expecting anyone but the watchman.

'Can't wait to see their faces,' said Private Hollings gleefully.

They were disappointed when the next boat also brought the Chief of Police, but soon cheered up when the supplies were unloaded.

'Cor, anybody'd think we were going to be here for six months,' one of the men shouted approvingly.

'We'd have to set up a distillery if we did. Don't think I can last six days without alcohol,' said another, and there was a chorus of agreement.

However it turned out that the Chief of Police had brought several crates of beer of which he took charge, promising a ration each day for everyone. A thoughtful man, he had also brought a football and a couple of packs of playing cards.

Not knowing when the scientists would be coming it was important to keep a look-out, and not show much light at night, but the watchman seemed very definite about 'next week' so they should not have long to wait.

They created a makeshift football pitch and 'Soppy' Martin (not a great athlete) wandered about on the hillside. He admired the yellow-green leaves of the local flora (so gentle compared to the primary colours on show on Fundador) and dug up some plants to grow outside the local barracks. His mates shook their heads. 'He'll be putting up net curtains next.'

Back on Fundador, the Governor, Mr Enrico and Mr Branco waited impatiently. They were all convinced that Mr Tonado was involved since he was approaching everyone to support his Bill, and seemed in a totally unnecessary state of excitement over something which would be of little concern to him in the normal way.

If he was involved, what about the Dane with whom he had been in earnest conversation up at the cemetery? Or there might be someone else.

The watchman was held in the garrison prison, so as not to cause any speculation, and the few soldiers remaining in the garrison were not allowed to go into town. A few beers in the local bars and the secret would be out.

'One good thing is that when we do bring back these people, anyone mixed up with it on Fundador can't get away. Meanwhile it's still top secret. We don't want anyone warning the people so that we never catch them - don't you agree?' said the Governor.

They did, and to all intents and purposes Fundador continued in its peaceful and placid fashion.

After the seventh day had passed since the enterprise was started it began to seem likely that the scientists had somehow been warned. Corporal Duckworth asked his CO, and the Chief of Police asked the Chief Minister, whether it might not be wise for them to return to Fundador. They could always keep an eye on the place and surprise them if they did turn up.

But whilst this was being considered, on the eighth night, the news came through. The Chief of Police told the governor first.

'We've got them. No-one hurt. Better send another boat. Six scientists and - you won't believe this - Colonel Amstrad!'

'Good God!'

'And a crate of monkeys.' The Chief of Police was enjoying himself.

'I should think you could leave those behind,' said the Governor. 'They'll be happy enough there. Only wish they knew how lucky they are.'

'I've questioned Amstrad. In fact I persuaded him we knew he had two accomplices on the island and it is

Mr Tonado and the trainee at the hotel. He gave in quite easily. I think we can safely leave them until I get back.'

The Governor understood that though he might be asked to help he must not interfere, so he agreed. He would send the boat off right away and keep quiet about it all. 'You've told your Government?'

'I'm about to ring the Chief Minister and he'll tell Mr Branco and Mr Enrico. No-one else until I've arrested the other two.'

Returning ahead of the army the Chief of Police brought with him the scientists and a morose Colonel Amstrad. The latter's efforts to convince the Chief of Police that his intentions were purely humanitarian, and that he had been stopped from doing the greatest service to the world, got him nowhere.

Once on Fundador the Chief of Police was somewhat flummoxed. Amstrad began complaining about invasion of his civil rights. Saying that he and the scientists had done nothing and could not be held made some sense. The Chief Minister, in consultation with the Governor, concluded that there was little they could be charged with, and anyway there was not enough accommodation at the police station for them all. And how about the Danish connection at the hotel? Things began to get tricky, the Chief Minister saying that if he had been informed immediately the scientists turned up he would have suggested letting the experimental station on Assandra get under way and then arrest everyone concerned with it. Then they would have had a case.

For the moment the 'prisoners' were put up in the hotel. Amstrad's nephew was horrified that his uncle should have behaved in this way and barred him from his suite. Amstrad in fact just wished to return home and he was prepared to create as much fuss as possible until he was allowed off the island. He pointed out that since Assandra belonged to no-one, neither Fundador nor the British had any jurisdiction over what went on there. Becoming rather cocky, the scientists joined Amstrad in his campaign and their spokesman said he wished to bring an action against the Chief of Police, the Governor and anyone else they cared to mention for the theft of the monkeys. He also enquired what kind of counselling services existed on Fundador since he and his colleagues were suffering from shock after the treatment they had so unexpectedly received.

The Governor was not very pleased at this stage to receive an urgent message from Eustace Proctor to the effect that he wished to speak to him on a most delicate matter, of interest to HM Government if not 'the gracious lady herself'.

Mr Proctor arrived at Government House with a string bag from which he took a battered history of Fundador, which he opened at a page previously marked by a decaying invitation to a Hunt Ball which the Governor could not help noticing was dated 1947. Mr Proctor pointed to a paragraph which stated that under the original Treaty handing Fundador over to the United Kingdom mention was made, in brackets, of the 'worthless Atoll Assandra'. It belonged to Fundador!

Various people said that of course they had known this all along. They had only to be asked. People remembered their grandfathers mentioning it - or was it their great uncles?

The clouds cleared. A case of trespass was brought and because of the serious intentions behind it, both to break the law through experiments on live animals and to make millions of pounds through subsequent research - 'But it would all have gone to Fundador' pleaded Amstrad - very heavy fines were levied on all the conspirators, and once these had been paid all but Mr Tonado must leave the island and never return. The shame was such that Mr Tonado left anyway, still professing his innocence (not backed up by the Dane at the hotel), and at the same time cursing the Fundador establishment for its short-sightedness in letting such a source of income slip though its hands. He swore that once the project had got going the Chief Minister and House of Representatives were to be informed. They, however, were greatly satisfied with the amount raised in fines and there was much argument as to what should be done with it. The police felt they deserved a large whack, as did the Tourist Department. Even the Governor suggested that some compensation for the army's involvement might be fair. The Chief Librarian was convinced that the library should get the lion's share since the book from which Mr Proctor had quoted was one he had taken out from the library some fifteen years previously. Unkindly, they sent Mr Proctor a lengthy summary of the fines he had incurred by keeping the book for so long.

In the end the Chief Minister declared that, like all such monies, it should go to the Treasury and the Treasury should make grants to all the parties involved, which they did.

The island was agog at all these revelations and many ex-pats were delighted by the fall from grace of Mrs

Bryce's protégé, Jens Amstrad. Needless to say their delight was short-lived. From what Marjorie told the Bridge Club and the Bridge Club told anyone who cared to listen, she had been the prime mover in the whole Amstrad affair. She had reported the meeting between Mr Tonado and the Dane from the hotel and all along she had realised there might be an Amstrad connection. 'There was always something a little, shifty shall we say, about him.' And of course she had taken a back seat while the matter was being investigated by those in authority. Far be it from her to push herself forward in any way. So now it had to be admitted on all sides that Marjorie Bryce was an exceptional lady and that her MBE was deserved.

'Well,' said the Governor to his wife, 'she did start the ball rolling so perhaps she should get the credit. I expect she really believes she came to me with suspicions rather than irritation at the reaction of Mr Tonado over the bird-watching observation post. Perhaps she should be made a Dame?'

'Why not crown her Queen of Fundador,' said his wife, with unusual asperity.

'She'd carry it off, you know,' he said, rather proudly as if she were some invention of his own.

When Jens Amstrad heard of Marjorie's involvement his admiration for her knew no bounds. He wrote to congratulate her and to explain the goodness of his intentions. 'Consider, dear lady, if you or your devoted sister should ever display the signs of Alzheimer - and no-one is immune - would you not have blessed the day that I, Jens Amstrad, had carried out the experiments and research which would have relieved all the symptoms? I shall not return to Fundador, nor will my wife. My nephew will run the hotel and I have his promise that our suite will forever be at your disposal for your family and friends. Farvel JA.'

Marjorie was pleased with this missive, though both she and Molly would have preferred no reference to Alzheimer's Disease coupled with their names. It caused them a certain amount of distress whenever they forgot a name or a much-used telephone number - and those British postal codes. Marjorie was at pains to blame Molly for interrupting her with idle chatter, and Molly would flush and say she was sorry, she did hope she wasn't going 'a bit - well - you know.'

'You did forget the bread yesterday, and the spoons for dessert at supper - but don't worry, my dear, you have a long way to go yet.' The implication that she had started on the road to senility was not comforting, but in the general excitement of the events on Fundador they soon let the subject fade into the background.

Passing the Barracks, Marjorie noticed an attractive plant with greeny-yellow leaves. Perfect backing for her crimson dahlias. She asked for a cutting, announcing grandly that she had 'green fingers'. 'Help yourself, lady,' said Corporal Duckworth, glancing at her hands. All he noticed was that they were certainly not gardener's hands. Nevertheless, and needless to say, the cutting took instantly, and soon the front garden of Villa Marmol became the envy of the cul-de-sac. She promised cuttings, but none were forthcoming.

Marjorie's post had increased to the extent that the postman suggested Matty should meet him on his afternoon rounds, which took him to the other side of town, so that he could pass the next batch of letters over to her. He had a very soft spot for Matty, and she was only too delighted to go on this important errand. She delivered the letters into Marjorie's hands one at a time, muttering unintelligibly over each, studying them back and front.

At first Marjorie received official letters. A citation from the League Against Cruel Sports (which seemed perhaps misplaced), a certificate from the Anti-Vivisection League and another from an organisation which lobbied against the use of live animals for research. Greenpeace wrote to her, and the RSPCA sent her a medal. Once the British press got hold of the story then her mail came from the general public, admiring this stalwart English lady who had stood out against cruelty to animals - they had an idea that the Fundadorans were all for it, but since the Fundadorans didn't see the letters it did not really matter.

Once the newspapers reached the library, Marjorie would have been obliged to queue up with the ex-pats to see them, but the librarian promised to send them up to Villa Marmol each evening. The headlines were confusing. *The Daily Telegraph* gave a fairly accurate account, on the basis of Marjorie's claim to have unmasked the plot, and headed it 'ENGLISH WOMAN FOILS ANIMAL EXPERIMENTERS'. The headline in *The Daily Mail* was 'EXPERIMENTS ON LIVE ANIMALS THWARTED - IS THIS THE TIP OF THE ICEBERG?' Their fearless investigative journalists would leave no stone unturned. *The Sun* splashed the headline 'MAJESTIC MARGE SEES OFF DEVILISH DANE' over the front page, and even Marjorie had to admit to Molly that the story inside was somewhat embroidered.

Some of the 'intrepid' reporters flew to the mainland and came over on the steamer to interview Marjorie, and she had her photograph taken looking out to sea at the Pets' Graveyard - a second photograph was taken of her overseeing Molly as she removed a splinter from a dog's foot at the Shelter. When asked her age she smiled haughtily and said 'I have always done my duty at every age.' They described her as a pensioner and she wished she had told them she was in her fifties, but she had somehow imagined that they would see her younger than that, perhaps 'forty something'; however such a minor set back did not concern her for long. The reports exaggerated wonderfully her exploits. She had nursed dying Assandrians, arranged for medical help, sat up all night in the hospital seeing them to their ends. She had observed with horror the plight of the animals on Fundador (this was not appreciated by those Fundadorans who could read English). She had educated the populace and they now looked after their pets most beautifully. She would soon be turning her attention to the donkeys. A photograph was taken of Belle, erect and haughty with Marjorie. Then there was her MBE and the inaccurate news that her suggestion for a Bird Observation Post on Assandra had been agreed by the House of Representatives.

As a result of this the Fundadoran Department of Tourism received endless enquiries from bird-watchers and bemusedly concluded that Assandra it should be, chalets and all. Developing the bay, building the chalets - in the circumstances perhaps they could use the pre-fab material set up by the scientists on the other side of the island - and the Observation Post could now be paid for easily from tourist income, and would lead to much more. Besides, now that Assandra was known to belong to Fundador it didn't seem quite so remote. In fact a place to be proud of.

The ex-pats and the educated Fundadorans grumbled a good deal over the exaggerated reports of Marjorie's exploits, but Marjorie said at the Bridge Club 'Whoever believes a word they read in the newspapers? They didn't get it from me. Nurse dying Assandrians indeed!' Once these remarks had circulated people nodded their heads. 'Such a wise lady.' Of course she ignored the rubbish written about her. In fact Marjorie revelled in it, though she was not too happy to see that the Whalleys and Mrs Turtle had sold their stories to the press. The Whalleys told *The Independent* and *The Sunday Express* that they had known the sisters intimately, ever since they had themselves moved to Bournemouth, and always admired the way they had devoted themselves to their parents. Such a burden, stoically borne. And how delighted they had been when, after their parents' deaths, the sisters had married. And more in the same vein.

Meanwhile Mrs Turtle spoke to *The Daily Mail*. She had read the Whalleys' account in the library, where she went to read all the newspapers when there had been a nasty murder or some equally exciting event, and she managed to rubbish the Whalleys. Her ladies had never spoken to the Whalleys - not the same class. (The Whalleys were furious at this, assuming Mrs Turtle meant that those dreary women were a cut above them). Mrs Turtle managed to rake up a few incidents where Marjorie threw a nut to a squirrel, or made encouraging sounds to a cat.

Marjorie would have been mollified had she known that Mrs Whalley had gone to great pains to look her best for a photograph but when she suggested it the cheeky reporter had said 'Thanks love, not today.'

Once the photographs of Marjorie at the Cemetery and Shelter were published she was assured of a regular correspondence from the UK. She was regarded as the Marge Proops of the pet world and the fact that the answers to their pet queries came from such a great distance gave them an extra quality. Molly would be sent to the library to look up information in the books on pet care, obtained from the UK, and Marjorie would study British magazines such as *The Field* and *Country Life*, and her public was so satisfied that eventually she was offered a regular Question and Answer page in a British women's magazine, where she regurgitated information gleaned from other UK magazines. The irony of it all escaped her, and she accepted Molly's admiration and description of her to her local friends as 'a journalist' without a qualm. She was certainly glad of the money she was paid by the magazine as she was finding postage something of a burden.

Fortunately Roy Bryce and Archie Jessop were difficult to track down and by the time the press found the former the story had died. Roy was slightly disappointed as he had intended saying that Marjorie was an under-sexed pain in the neck, but in retrospect he thought it was as well left unsaid. When a cub reporter finally came up with Archie, and put him on the alert, his boss eyed him sadly. 'So far as we're concerned, laddie Marjorie Bryce is dead.' The reporter was still young enough to think he must tie up loose ends, so he passed the news on to Archie.

'Dead?' barked Archie.

'Well, a dead issue,' explained the reporter.

'Just my bloody luck,' grumbled Archie, over a pint at his local.

Eleven

As things quietened down, Marjorie began to think about her award. She had the option of taking it from the Governor or of going back to England and receiving it from the Queen. She had been given a date if she wished to go Buckingham Palace.

'I think I should receive it from the Queen,' she said to Molly.

'Oh Marjorie, that would be wonderful. After all it won't happen again - at least, I shouldn't think so. A trip home would be nice, and we could see Emily and Alma.' Molly was thoroughly excited by the prospect.

'Yes, I believe that is the right thing to do. I must go to the travel agent tomorrow and see when the next cruise ship is coming in. Then we might fly back to the mainland and take the steamer over as there certainly won't be a cruise ship which could bring us back after a week in England. We don't want to stay longer than that.'

'I've never flown,' said Molly in a tone of awe. 'Well, neither have you. It would be exciting.'

'I daresay, but we couldn't afford anything but the economy class and I'm told it's very cramped. But needs must - ' Marjorie put a brave face on it.

They found that a cruise ship would be calling in at Fundador on its way back to the UK just in time to get them there before the investiture, and Mina Caleta at Fundador Travel told them that by a lucky chance there were two seats available on a return flight on Eagle Airlines. Marjorie booked them into a small hotel in London, just off Sloane Street, which she felt suitably respectable, and Molly wrote to Emily. She had written to the aunts when she read the reports in the papers and longed to hear the story first hand, and the thought of being able to see Marjorie receive her award was an added joy.

Travelling home on the ship was very different from coming out. The Captain had been asked by the Governor to look after them and they sat at his table in the dining room, Marjorie on his right and Molly opposite. If anything was needed to confirm to Marjorie that she had arrived this was it. She and Molly entered the dining room precisely five minutes after the appointed time of a meal. The Captain and the men present stood whilst Marjorie took her chair, assisted by the waiter. Molly meanwhile sat down, beaming at everyone.

On the first night the Captain introduced Marjorie to the rest of the table as the lady who had uncovered a plot to build an illegal experimental station on an island near Fundador, and she was regarded from then on as a Miss Marple. Her opinion was sought on various mysterious happenings in the lives of those present and it was surprising how many unsolved mysteries there were, perhaps somewhat exaggerated for effect. Marjorie would look judicious and she developed a good line in Delphic responses.

Molly was regarded as slightly simple which was unfair, but she found the kindness with which she was treated very pleasant and did not suspect she was being patronised.

As on their first voyage, Marjorie kept aloof from deck games and evening entertainments, only making an exception when the Captain asked her to present the ping-pong prize and help judge the fancy dress competition. Molly played deck quoits and bingo, and helped people to make their fancy dress costumes.

Unlike their first voyage the days sped by and all too soon, Molly felt, they were docking in Southampton. The rain and overcast sky didn't dampen their spirits. After all they were here for a special occasion. But when that rare figure, a porter, approached them and said cheerfully 'Welcome home, ladies,' both were taken aback to realize this was no longer their home.

Meanwhile, in Fundador, Mrs Hobson-Jones's husband was somewhat surprised when he saw coca leaves sprouting in his garden. Years in the Colonial Police had taken him all over the world and he was well up in drugs. His wife explained, with some relish, that she had taken a cutting from Marjorie's garden. 'After all, she promised. So we've all done it!'

Her husband looked thoughtful. His afternoon stroll took him up to the Villa Marmol and he was able to confirm that the ladies had indeed stolen a march on Mrs Bryce. Each boasted a nice new coca plant. He called at the Villa Marmol and met Matty at the door. He admired the plant. 'Soldiers - soldiers give it - ' she kissed her fingertips and waved them towards the town. He thanked her and made his way down town and to the barracks, and there he perceived even more of these desirable plants. A little gentle probing revealed that they came from Assandra. 'Had lots of enquiries,' said the Colonel. 'We're thinking of potting up cuttings for the Cathedral Fête - not many new plants around. One of our chaps, Private Martin, he's very good with plants. Did you want a cutting?' 'Thank you, no,' said Mr

Hobson-Jones and duly delivered his information to the Governor.

The Governor and the Chief Minister felt slightly at a disadvantage. Neither had been by the barracks recently, nor up to Marjorie's part of town, but secretly wondered whether they would have recognised the coca leaves in any case.

At a meeting between the Governor, the Chief Minister, Mr Branco and Mr Enrico it was decided to get hold of a good weedkiller from the mainland. Before the week was out a strange disease appeared to have struck the new plants. At the barracks 'Soppy' was inconsolable, and up at the villa Matty threw up her hands in dismay. What would her lady say?

Mrs Hobson-Jones was sure that she had seen a stealthy figure stealing up the cul-de-sac after dark. She had shouted to her husband to come and look. 'A man in black - creeping, peering into the gardens. Look, he's carrying something and - .' 'Come along, my dear. You know I don't like you snooping. Probably Matty's boyfriend.' And he took her by the arm. 'There's that rubbishy soap you like to watch just coming on.' Mrs Hobson-Jones was duly distracted, but next day, seeing all those dead plants, she wondered. Her husband told her not to worry her head about it, he'd seen they were poisonous anyway. 'Better without them. I like a nice dahlia myself.' And Mrs Hobson-Jones was consoled and secretly rather excited in anticipation of Mrs Bryce's reaction to the loss of her plant. She would never know of the thefts, and of this Mrs Hobson-Jones and her neighbours were rather glad.

Unknown to the islanders the same mystery figure had been at work on Assandra and all evidence of the coca plant had disappeared. The Governor and the Chief Minister decided not to pursue Amstrad - no longer with the UN in any case - and Mr Tonado. They were gone and no scandal attached to the island.

'I think they were pretty naive,' said the Governor. 'I suppose Amstrad did want to do experiments of some sort - he is a doctor after all - but cocaine smuggling! They wouldn't sell the leaves, there's not much money in that. So the lab would make up the basic paste and sell it to the dealers to process and sell to the drug barons. Probably imagined the dealers would be like jolly traders, take the paste and hand over the money, so Amstrad could do more expensive experiments.'

'They knew no-one from here bothers with Assandra so Mrs Bryce was certainly a fly in the ointment - in the paste you might say.' The Chief Minister, usually a little on his dignity when at Government House, allowed himself to smile.

'They couldn't be certain no-one would ever go there - a troop exercise for example.'

'Indeed. Naive is right, which makes me sure they hadn't made contact with anyone in the drugs business. They thought it would all be very simple. However once they had made contact - well, they would have been lucky to get away with their lives.' The Chief Minister was serious again.

'So we really did them a good turn.'

'That is very true. And now we can concentrate on the Bird Sanctuary - the Representatives are in general very keen.'

'I always said Mrs Bryce was worth her weight in gold,' said the Governor. He had a sudden vision of Marjorie taking a nostalgic trip on a fishing boat to

Assandra, and being held for ransom by drug barons, taming them of course, and - This would not do. Relief at danger past was making him light-headed. He smiled. 'Let's go onto the veranda,' and he led the Chief Minister into the cool of the evening. His wife, cutting a few flowers in the garden, came to join them. 'You both look very pleased with yourselves. I thought it might be something serious.'

'No, no. Just a little hiccup. Which suggests a drink - ' he really must control this unseemly levity - 'What will you have, Minister?'

Neither Marjorie nor Molly had realised how used they had become to the Fundadoran climate. They found it chilly and were glad to get to the hotel so that they could visit Peter Jones and buy warm cardigans. There were also the hats for the investiture. Molly must wear a small one so that people could see over her head.

'I prefer a small one myself,' said Marjorie. 'This is not an occasion for ostentation.' She chose a close fitting navy blue hat to match her navy suit, with a small white piece of braid in front, to go with her white blouse. She had advised Molly against her pleated flowered silk dress. 'You don't want to be overdressed, like those people at garden parties,' said Marjorie, 'all those pleats and ruffles and inappropriate shoes. Simplicity is the thing. I read in *Woman* the other day that it's considered bad form to overdress.'

'And to hyphenate your name,' said Molly brightly, having read the same article.

'And what would you hyphenate yours to, my dear Molly?' Marjorie asked witheringly.

'I only meant - well, sometimes things are done, and then later they're not done - and it must be very confusing, when people are trying to do the right thing - or - ' Molly floundered.

'Now, Molly, just forget all that and try on this hat.'

Sadly Marjorie could not have more than two family guests at the investiture so it had to be Molly and Emily. Alma was stoic and said she didn't mind. The mother of her best friend at school, June Garland, had been saying she would take the girls to the Zoo one day and this would be the perfect opportunity, if it suited Mrs Garland, which it did.

It was arranged that Emily and Alma would stay the night at the hotel with Marjorie and Molly, and see them off at Gatwick the next day, so Mrs Garland would bring Alma to the hotel around tea time.

This seemed a good plan and three days later Emily arrived at the hotel at nine-thirty in the morning, looking pretty in a pink cotton dress, with a white coat and shoes, and a pink hat.

Molly said 'You look lovely,' and Marjorie said 'I think we will all pass muster. Get your hat on Molly, we want to be early so that you get a front seat. You don't want to sit at the back.'

'And we must see the loo,' laughed Emily.

'Whatever for?' asked Marjorie, stopping in her tracks.

'You can go now, before we set out,' said Molly sensibly.

'It's just that someone told me it was so magnificent you have to see it. I suppose it's old fashioned and ornate.'

'With a pull up handle, and gold fittings,' said Molly excitedly, getting into the spirit of it all.

'And gold taps, and soap made from attar of roses, whatever that is,' said Emily giggling.

Marjorie was becoming impatient. 'Your hat, Molly,' and she shooed her out of the room. Molly was still giggling as she went and Marjorie said to Emily 'She's over-excited. You mustn't encourage her.'

Emily composed herself and promised she wouldn't.

There was a slight drizzle as they set off for the Palace. They did not mind and Marjorie said 'So like dear old England.'

The hotel doorman saw them into their taxi under a large black umbrella, and having heard Marjorie tell the driver where they were going said 'My regards to the Queen!' Marjorie, considering this lèse Majesté, gave him a repressive look.

Joining the queue in The Mall they felt rather grand until some youths scowled at them and shouted 'bloody toffs', and made rude gestures through the window. Emily and Molly were mortified but Marjorie just said 'People like that should be ignored. It's only jealousy. A very unpleasant characteristic.'

'Jealous of you?' asked Molly.

'Of what I stand for. Of the Monarchy, of honours,' said Marjorie, pushing an imaginary straying hair beneath her neat hat.

Emily said quietly 'I think it's money too. When you haven't much you always imagine everyone else has plenty. I remember feeling like that when Bernard left. Then I thought, well, we can just manage and I'll keep everything clean and tidy - so as to keep up our morale - and you can get really good clothes from Oxfam - '

Marjorie was horrified 'Second-hand?'

'Probably third or fourth,' laughed Emily. 'I always washed them or took them to be cleaned. The funny thing was the woman across the road kept saying things like 'It's all right for you' when we were both queuing for the same allowance. Yet she had a husband - a window cleaner, in regular work.'

'It doesn't seem fair that you both got the same when he was working. How can they allow it?' Molly asked innocently.

'I don't expect they knew,' said Emily. 'He wouldn't have told them.'

Molly said again, 'I think it's very unfair.'

'You must have noticed that life is unfair a good deal of the time,' said Marjorie. She wondered whether to pass on her copy of *The Game of Life and How to Play It* to Molly. Perhaps it would only confuse her.

At which point they forgot such mundane topics as they swept - crawled actually, Emily had to admit to Alma afterwards - through the gates into the courtyard of Buckingham Palace.

As they entered the Palace they were enchanted by the pictures and the cabinets full of glorious porcelain, and Emily noted the decor so as to be able to give Alma a full description. The recipients of honours were directed one way, guests the other. Looking at Molly and thinking of all she had done for other people Emily thought this was certainly one area of unfairness, although one which would not occur to Marjorie. How many of the guests were just as deserving as the recipients? But all of them looked as happy and proud as if it were they who were being honoured, and Emily saw what pleasure Marjorie's award was bringing Molly and she was proud of them both.

They didn't have to look for the loo as it was offered to them and they gazed at the fixtures and fittings with awe. Then they washed their hands with 'royal' soap, and dried them on 'royal' towels, and felt duly sanctified and ready to face the Queen.

They were in the front row and were able to watch the final preparations.

A sudden panic gripped Molly. 'Oh Emily, she didn't practise her curtsy!'

Emily smiled. 'Don't worry, Molly dear, I expect Aunt Marjorie was born knowing how to curtsy.'

Very quietly, the Queen and her courtiers came into the ballroom and without fuss she stood on the small dais, 'as close to us as the head waiter' said Molly to Alma when they were having dinner that evening. They could not believe it, though from their wonderful position in the centre of the front row it was bound to be so. The most exciting thing was that they could hear every word which the Queen spoke to the recipients as she pinned on the medals and handed over the boxes in which they would be kept except for special occasions.

When Marjorie came through the door on the left she walked calmly forward until she reached the spot where the Queen was standing, turned and curtsied, Molly almost fainted with emotion. She was so overwhelmed she did not hear what the Queen said. After a few seconds Marjorie turned and went out through the door on the right, just as if she had been to the Palace often and knew her way about, Molly thought.

Meeting afterwards, Marjorie confirmed to Emily that the Queen had said 'I believe you are very fond of dogs?' To which Marjorie had replied 'Indeed I am, Your

Majesty.' 'Me too,' said Her Majesty, and 'I admire the work you have done on Fundador.'

'What did you say then?' asked Molly.

'Why, naturally I said "Thank you, Ma'am".'

Molly sighed happily. Thank goodness it was Marjorie, who could be relied on not to let the family down. Molly doubted whether she herself would have been able to say a word.

It was all over so quickly they couldn't believe it had really happened, so they were glad to find freelance photographers outside the Palace, keen to take their photographs. Molly and Emily stood on either side of Marjorie, who held up her medal, now neatly replaced in its box, and the photographer asked if Marjorie would like a copy of the photo sent to her and the local press. He was not phased by Fundador and said he would send his bill with the photographs. 'I can always tell Her Majesty if you don't pay!' he joked. A joke in poor taste Marjorie considered.

Next day Emily and Alma went with them on the train to Gatwick, so as to help with their suitcases.

'I'm glad you didn't bring the cabin trunk,' laughed Alma. 'Do you remember?'

'It seems such a long time ago,' said Molly. 'So much has happened.'

'And now the life we are going back to is one we know, which is a great comfort.'

'It *is* your life now,' said Emily. 'And it's lovely for us to imagine you both there.'

'And you'll come and visit us again soon, won't you?' said Molly.

'Whenever we can,' promised Emily.

'I never want to visit anywhere else,' said Alma fervently. 'If you see Tessie give her my love. And Amos, and Matty. Oh, everyone. I miss them all so much.'

'Of course we will,' said Molly affectionately.

'Now come along,' said Marjorie. 'We must put these cases on a trolley and let you go or you'll miss your train.'

After fond goodbyes Molly and Marjorie started a trek around the airport looking for the Eagle Airlines desk. Finally Marjorie told Molly to sit with the trolley whilst she made another tour of the desks. Eventually she found it, behind and to the side of the other well-known airlines, and a very makeshift desk it was too. Several people were waiting in a queue but the girl behind the desk was in no hurry to take their baggage. She was making up her face. Then she practised her smile, and removed some lipstick from her front teeth. She fussed around with papers on her desk and finally looked up.

'I can take your luggage now,' she said, giving them the benefit of her enigmatic smile, 'but I'm afraid there will be a four-hour delay. Your plane is on its way from Frankfurt, and it will have to be serviced. However,' she went on, as if reading from a script, 'this will not inconvenience you since we will give you vouchers for a snack and a cup of coffee, and you will be able to look around the shops and choose your favourite magazines from the news-stand. Thank you - ' and she snatched the ticket and passport from the hands of the first person in the queue. The whole transaction was so quickly over that no-one did more than grumble as if they were waiting for an overdue bus. However when Marjorie reached the desk she demanded to know why the plane was coming from Frankfurt. 'Are you sure there is a plane? Does this company actually exist?'

'Indeed it does,' smiled the girl, 'and the plane is on its way, and it will be available for our flight in - well, in less than four hours.' She said this as though doing Marjorie a great favour.

'Yes,' said Marjorie, 'three hours and fifty-five minutes. This is gross inefficiency and I will report the whole matter to your Managing Director.'

'May I have your ticket, Madam?' said the cheerful girl. And 'No, I'm afraid we cannot book seats.'

The girl's smile was permanent - 'Like an advertisement for toothpaste,' Marjorie snorted, which pleased the by now admiring audience of their fellow travellers. 'Sock it to 'em,' said a red-faced man at her elbow. 'Do you mind,' said Marjorie, pushing him to one side. 'You tell 'em,' said a fat lady on her other side. Marjorie continued to do so and the girl continued to smile.

'Your flight will be announced and it will be on the board, there will be no need to make enquiries,' said the girl as if imparting some pleasant news. 'Bon appetit!' At which the telephone on her desk rang, saving her further harassment from Marjorie. 'Oh yes,' she said into the mouthpiece, 'I'm the same. My lot have been delayed four hours. Yes, they are. You know how it is. Yes, all of them really. Well, some more than others ...'

Marjorie and Molly moved away in search of the cafeteria, and in due course the red-faced man and the fat lady appeared, and were joined by other passengers. The fat lady sat at the next table to Marjorie and Molly and the red-faced man close by. Marjorie felt haunted. She complained at the counter about the dirty table and was given a cloth to wipe it down. She complained about the strength of the tea and was handed two more tea bags.

'It's a disgrace,' she said. 'An utter disgrace - '

'They treat us like muck. We're paying and they treat us like muck,' said the fat lady.

'Like cattle,' said the red-faced man.

'I can hardly bear it,' said Marjorie. 'This Greek chorus plus Eagle Airlines. Truly a nightmare.'

'This bun is nice,' said Molly placatingly.

Marjorie hit hers with a fork. 'Hard as nails,' she said.

'Like muck -

'Cattle -

'Come along Molly, we'll be better off in the airport shop.' There she had the pleasure of telling the assistant that their bargain perfumes were exactly the same price as at Harrods. She had never actually been to Harrods, but she had read in a magazine that this was the case.

Somehow time passed. They sat, they stood, they walked; they looked at all the shops and they bought a copy of *The Lady*. Their flight was finally called.

The same smiling girl was at the entrance to the departure lounge, now wearing a kind of forage cap which did not match the rest of her uniform. She checked their boarding cards and saw them through the hand luggage inspection, and finally took them on what Marjorie later described as a cross-country hike to their plane. They had to board from the back, and scramble for the seats they felt safest, or farthest from the smokers who were allowed in the back four rows.

Finally settled, a pleasant female voice over the intercom gave them instructions on what to do if the plane crashed on land or in the sea, or if the oxygen supply was cut off. A smiling stewardess demonstrated the procedures as if they were part of a fun day in Disneyland. Molly was horrified. Up to now she had never thought of such things, and she didn't know whether this was a special warning for passengers on this flight because of some doubt as to the plane's airworthiness, or whether they said this on all flights. She longed to ask Marjorie, but how would *she* know?

The voice over the intercom now announced that there would be a delay in taking off as the food had not yet been delivered.

Ten minutes later a man's voice told them that the food had arrived. However there would be a further delay as the pilot was busy with paperwork. It seemed strange that on coming in from Frankfurt he should have been obliged to do office work, but they were now all prisoners of Eagle Airlines and must accept anything they were told. After a little soft music the female voice returned to assure them that the pilot was doing his best but there was some misunderstanding and he was being asked to pay the fuel bill in full before taking off. 'He's raising the money,' she said sweetly.

Passengers were becoming restive. A voice from the back shouted 'I suppose you want a whip round?'

Another voice called out 'Is there a pilot in the house?' and above the laughter were cries of 'What a shambles' - 'Like muck' - 'Cattle'.

Marjorie closed her eyes. Never again she vowed.

Molly nudged her. 'He's here,' she said, in soothing tones, and there indeed was the pilot; in jeans, T-shirt and baseball cap. He smiled, waved at the passengers and strolled into the cockpit.

'As soon as we get home I will write to the airline,' said Marjorie. 'It is a complete disaster,' and she closed her eyes again.

Molly said in a surprised voice 'Yes, home - it is home now, it really is,' and sank back contentedly into her seat as the plane taxied along the runway. But her pleasure was not to last long.

Once the plane was in the air the young man in front of her pushed his seat back as far as it would go, gave it a few extra pushes for good measure, and threw his greasy pony tail over the back of it, almost hitting Molly in the face. She was in the middle of her row and completely wedged in. The thought of ten hours like this, unable to move, with a pony tail dangling in front of her face and a baseball player piloting the plane was so appalling that even Molly's ability to see the bright side faltered.

The stewardess passed up and down the aisle with drinks to keep the passengers happy and then there was a meal. A menu with an eagle on the cover was handed to each passenger. It listed hors d'oeuvre, stir-fried seafood with straw mushrooms, braised mixed vegetables, fried rice with scallions, sole meunière, duck a l'orange, sautéed green peas, diced carrots with white radish, sautéed potatoes with onions, cheese and crackers, black forest gateau, roll and butter, chocolates, tea or coffee. Molly was overcome by it all and said to Marjorie 'I will never be able to eat all this - how embarrassing.'

Marjorie, having by now got the measure of this airline, told Molly not to worry. It was highly unlikely that this feast would materialise. The delivery of their plastic trays confirmed her view. Each tray was divided into minute sections, each containing a tasting of the items mentioned, a small space being left in the centre for the main course. The ever smiling hostess asked 'Duck or fish?' and delivered a foil-covered carton which, when opened, gave forth a combined smell of duck and fish, so that it was left to the imagination of the diner to decide which it was. Marjorie and Molly both asked for duck, but Molly thought she had fish. Marjorie advised against eating any of it.

Coffee was served by a second smiling hostess who appeared unable to aim straight, so that her progress was punctuated by 'So sorry - so sorry.' Marjorie thanked her icily, but her expression never changed.

After this long drawn out snack their Captain told them they would be landing at Angachurka. This was a great surprise to the passengers who had never heard of Angachurka, let alone a stop off.

'How extraordinary,' said Marjorie. 'Fundador Travel never mentioned this. Really this airline - if one can call it that - is a truly Heath Robinson affair. And don't ask me who or what Heath Robinson was Molly or I'll scream!'

Molly gazed at her wide-eyed. Marjorie hadn't screamed since she was a child, when it had been a very rare and alarming occurrence as she had usually got her own way. The fact that Marjorie had even thought of screaming was enough to silence Molly.

They fastened their seat belts and Marjorie said no more for the moment. At the back of her mind was the feeling that she should have realised that a plane this size would hardly be likely to carry enough fuel for the whole flight. But she hadn't known what kind of plane it would be until they boarded it. That Mina Caleta at

Fundador Travel had made it sound rather special. Marjorie would not be surprised if Mr Tonado had something to do with Eagle Airlines, and it was going the same way as him. She would certainly find out as soon as they were back in Fundador.

On landing at Angachurka it took some time for steps of the right height to be found to release them from the plane and when at last they were in place the passengers found they had to negotiate a rather alarmingly steep first step. They were rallied by their stewardess, smiling as ever.

They followed her across the dusty landing strip and into a small building with two doors, one marked PERSONS and the other OFFICE PERSONS. Through the Persons door they found two rows of wooden benches to sit on, all facing the office, the upper part of which was glass. On one side of them was a counter selling bottled drinks, amazingly stored in a refrigerated container, and some dubious sweetmeats. On the other side a notice announced a space TO LET, though for what purpose it would be hard to imagine.

Marjorie said in a loud voice that the sweetmeats should not be touched with a barge pole. Unthinkingly Molly said 'Barge pole?' then covered her mouth apologetically. Marjorie kindly let her off with a nod of the head. Since they were sitting at the back of the room she was able to ignore those around her. She rested her head against the wall and closed her eyes.

There was desultory conversation. Some children whined and a baby screamed, and some more imaginative people took advantage of their understanding that TO LET had lost an I in the middle, and boldly entered the nearby door.

As the passengers gazed through the glass into the office they observed their baseball Captain in amiable conversation with two 'office persons'. There was much back slapping and shoulder shrugging and laughing, followed by the production of a bottle and glasses. Passengers might have grumbled at this, wondering what rules governed drink driving on aircraft, but feeling that they were in fact watching television, and that the Captain was just an actor they recognised, they gazed on. The scene had nothing to do with them. They might have been at home in front of their own sets, except that they would not have put up with hard wooden benches.

Fortunately there was fuel at this unlikely airstrip, and since nothing else was happening the refuelling was completed quite quickly. Marjorie opened her eyes to see, through the glass, the Captain handing over some papers to one of the officials, shaking hands warmly with each of them, and leaving by a side door to return to the plane.

Marjorie said, in some surprise, 'This is the only efficient thing which has happened since we reached Gatwick. We have a lot to learn from the Third World. I will certainly mention that in my letter to the airline. Thank goodness there was no problem about money - I can't think how he would have been able to raise money here.'

'They probably trust him,' said Molly, impressed by the laughter and handshakes.

'Birds of a feather,' said Marjorie, which wasn't quite what Molly had meant, but she was pondering over the Third World. If this was the Third where were the First and Second Worlds, and what about Heaven?

'Come along everyone,' called the stewardess, as if to a group of primary school children. 'Wasn't it fun? Good to stretch your legs and to see new places.' All they could see outside was the airstrip and a sandy road, the trees on either side of it growing more dense as it narrowed and faded into the distance. 'Don't leave anything behind as we don't know when we'll be here again.'

'I'll bet,' said a man whom Molly recognised as the one sitting on her left on the plane.

Back on board this sceptic instantly fell asleep. The man in front of Molly once more banged his seat and threw his pony tail over the back of it. But Molly felt she could now survive. It was like all suffering. Bad while it lasted but giving you a new appreciation of life when it was over.

'It just shows that one should pay attention to one's instincts,' said Marjorie. 'I had a feeling that I should not trust such an inexperienced girl as Mina Caleta. How could she know about airlines? It was difficult to say anything when her father is so kind to us over special cuts of meat in his shop. My suspicions were aroused when she said we were lucky to be able to get seats at such short notice. I will write to the Chairman.' She already had stationery printed with Mrs Marjorie Bryce MBE at the top. He would realise she was not just any ignorant package traveller. And if he offered her a free trip by way of compensation she would have great pleasure in turning it down. She would be writing on behalf of her fellow passengers and perhaps those to follow - if the airline continued to exist. As a representative of the Queen this would be her rôle, and she was proud of it. She would read the newspapers each day thoroughly and espouse causes on behalf of 'the man in the street' - or was it 'on the Clapham omnibus'? Well, if he wasn't in the street he was probably on a bus so it was all the same. Her mind drifted along these lines and she suddenly said to Molly 'I will need a word processor.'

Molly looked at her in amazement. 'I'm sure they don't provide that sort of thing,' she gasped, unable to visualise even a small portable typewriter on the flimsy table in front of Marjorie. And whatever was she going to type? Besides, she had never learned to type properly and it would be very undignified to type in front of everybody with two fingers, as she did at home.

Marjorie brought her up with a jolt. 'Really, Molly, you are sometimes totally unrealistic. Totally. I may need one at home, not at this precise moment.' She looked at Molly and wondered whether the flight was too much for her and she was getting delirious. She certainly looked extremely flushed.

'I think you should watch the film Molly. It will take your mind off things.'

Ever eager to please Molly did as she was told. For a while she watched the film, some man with a girl in tow foiling a large number of bad men out to destroy them. Like a tide, the villains surged forward until some booby trap, swiftly arranged by the hero, held them up. Again and again bad men fell by the wayside, only to reappear as if from an inexhaustible supply. It was confusing to have an old comedy show with canned laughter as a background to all this, and finally, taking off her earphones, Molly said 'I think it's easier to watch without the sound. It's so distracting, all that laughter.' Marjorie explained patiently that she must be on the wrong channel. 'Press the buttons until you get words which go with the picture,' she said, as if to a child. But Molly never managed it and, ending up with soft music, soon fell asleep.

Going to the lavatory before the plane landed, Marjorie and Molly passed through the smokers' zone. There was a pall of smoke over them and other passengers coughed as they penetrated the cloud.

On returning to their seats, Molly made a rare and modest joke. 'Not quite up to Buckingham Palace standards,' she said, looking sideways at Marjorie, not sure if this would be allowed.

Marjorie gave one of her equally rare snorting laughs. Molly was pleased.

As if to make up for this lapse Marjorie now spoke critically of the smoking area. 'We had to pass through it after all.' And the man on Molly's other side, who had been awakened by Marjorie's sharp snort said 'It's all part of a plan to kill off smokers. Get them all together so that they create this thick smoky atmosphere and choke to death. Department of Health and MI5 worked it out - ' His hope of eliciting a further snort from Marjorie was thwarted, and Molly looked horrified. 'Oh no, how dreadful,' she said. So he resisted the call of nature and went back to sleep.

Considering their pilot they made a very smooth landing Marjorie conceded. It was just a pity he didn't seem to know when to stop, taking them to all four corners of the airport before finally leaving them what seemed to be half a mile from the terminal. Marjorie had the impression that Eagle Airlines was not a valued customer of world airports.

As they left the plane the stewardesses stood on either side of the gangway, smiling as ever, repeating mechanically, 'I hope you enjoyed the flight.'

Marjorie passed by without a sideways glance, but Molly smiled and said 'Oh, yes. Yes indeed,' and tripped into Marjorie.

'Whatever are you doing Molly? Here, take this,' and Marjorie added her own cabin bag to Molly's.

'Thank you,' said Molly, always happy to be useful.

Their trek across the tarmac to the terminal was tiring after being cooped up so long, and it was very hot. Molly staggered a bit, but as she was behind Marjorie this went unnoticed. At the terminal door they peered around at the confusion which confronted them. People wandered to and fro aimlessly, and when Marjorie said loudly 'Baggage?' no-one took any notice. She went to a desk where an argument was taking place behind the counter. When she managed to attract attention the participants looked at her as if she were to blame for everything, but at least they both pointed in the same direction, which implied that the luggage from the plane would turn up on the far side of the building. To Molly's relief it did seem to be the right place. At least various people recognisable from the plane were hovering there, gazing at an empty conveyor belt which came through one set of decaying plastic curtains and disappeared through another.

When Marjorie was able to push Molly past the assembled passengers, so as to view the luggage which eventually began to pass before their eyes, it was some time before she heard Molly's cry of success. In fact at first Molly had seen the back view of her own suitcase disappearing through the second set of curtains and she had imagined that that was the end of it. Her case would be thrown into some lost luggage area never to be seen again. Marjorie was too far back to be questioned about this and just then Marjorie's case turned up. Molly put out a hand to grab it but the man next to her pushed forward for his bag and Marjorie's had gone. Molly was near to tears. How could she tell Marjorie? But suddenly, to her unbounded joy, her own case reappeared and the system became clear. The cases might seem to go from left to right but they just went round and round. How very clever. This time she was lucky and made a grab, nearly spraining her wrist. She caught the case, dragged it off the conveyor belt, and hauled it through the people around her.

'I've got it, Marjorie. I got it the second time round!' She was triumphant.

'What about mine?' said Marjorie. 'Have you seen it?'

'Well, yes. It's on its way. I'll just see how far it's got - ' and Molly pushed to the front again, only to see the case disappearing through the far curtains. How many chances did you get, she wondered anxiously. She was determined to stay put until everyone had gone before she would admit to Marjorie that she had let it go twice. Just when she was convinced it would never return, there it was. Oh joy! She grabbed it, spun on her toes as she dragged it off the turntable, hit the person next to her sharply on the knee and hauled it back to Marjorie.

'I think you've crippled someone, Molly. That lady looks a bit upset.'

For once Molly did not care. All she wanted to do was get out of this horrible place, get into a taxi, and go to the docks. Once they were on the steamer everything would be all right. Fundador time would operate and life would be back to normal.

Customs was the usual chaos and they found themselves in the queue of people with something to declare, although they did not realise this. Marjorie was infuriated to have questions barked at her in their incomprehensible language, and the snapping of fingers eager for their keys. She kept mouthing 'Nothing - no, nothing' and waving her hand across her face in a negative gesture, whilst the official carried on at great length, pointing to the sign above him and continuing to snap his fingers. In the end Marjorie handed him their keys disdainfully, and he groped through the boring contents of their cases and gesticulated to his neighbour, who shrugged and tapped his head. With a few more no doubt well chosen words the official handed back the keys to Marjorie, who seemed to be in charge, but she handed them on to Molly, who huffed and puffed and got the cases closed and locked.

'I told you yours was far too full,' said Marjorie. She was extremely irritated. Firstly because she blamed the customs officer for the fact that they ended up in the wrong queue - he should have realised at once that they were people worthy of special attention and should be in no queue at all - and secondly with herself for not having arranged for a taxi for their journey from the airport to the docks. Mina Caleta should have suggested it. Normally Marjorie did not regret her lack of foreign languages but today it seemed an insurmountable problem.

'Taxi!' she called out regally, but no-one took any notice. She then approached various uniformed persons and again said 'Taxi?' very loudly. They shrugged and pointed in different directions, and returned to their loud and apparently acrimonious conversations.

There had been no trolleys and they had had to drag their cases to the front entrance. Obviously Molly could not manage it by herself so Marjorie had to buckle to. It was all extremely tiresome. They placed their suitcases against the wall just outside the entrance and sat on them. Cars screeched to a halt, others set off with squealing tyres. People shouted, came together and parted, and generally behaved like a colony of ants. There seemed no purpose to their lives at all. Marjorie would shrill every now and then 'Taxi!' and Molly would echo her. But there was no response.

'All I can say is thank goodness we don't live on the mainland. Compared to this, Fundador is Paradise,' said Marjorie.

'And it's lucky the steamer doesn't leave for another two hours,' said Molly, pleased with herself for being so practical.

Marjorie closed her eyes.

Molly tried to see good in what was before her, but it was hard. Her head was throbbing and she was hungry. 'Shall I look for a sandwich?' she asked hopefully.

Marjorie, without opening her eyes, said 'Do you want to poison us, Molly?'

'No, no indeed.' Molly drooped.

'Now ladies,' boomed a cheerful voice, and before them stood the man who had slept so soundly next to Molly during the flight from London. 'Never say die. Someone not turned up? What's the problem?'

Molly got to her feet eagerly. 'We need a taxi. To go to the docks,' she said shyly, and Marjorie opened her eyes.

'The docks? That's where I'm going. Share my taxi - '
He let out a cry of 'Taxi' and three men ran forward. He chose one, indicated Marjorie's and Molly's suitcases, which the driver picked up, and they all went towards an old dented Chevrolet.

Marjorie was somewhat put out by the ease with which he got a taxi - or three if he had wanted them - whilst she had been ignored, and once in the taxi she said 'We were just resting our feet before calling for a taxi ourselves. However it is most kind of you to allow us to travel with you.' Thank goodness it's only a half-hour drive, she thought. She remembered this man's facetious comments about smokers and did not relish too much of his company.

'You girls going to Fundador?' he asked

Marjorie was furious by this mode of address and, drawing herself up as best she could from a sitting position, said haughtily: 'We live there.'

'Do you really? Your husbands work there?'

'I am Mrs Bryce, and this is my sister Mrs Jessop. We live together on Fundador.'

'My name's Grant - Robert Grant. I'm going there to set up some bird-watching complex. On a nearby island as I understand it.'

'Assandra,' said Marjorie. 'It was my idea in fact.' She threw this comment off casually, looking out of the window.

Mr Grant was impressed. 'You work for their Government?'

'Certainly not. I am an interested citizen,' said Marjorie grandly. 'I happen to have a certain amount of influence with the Chief Minister - '

'Marjorie discusses her ideas with the Governor,' broke in Molly proudly.

'Perhaps you could give me the benefit of your views on this bird-watching project, Mrs Bryce? Where is Assandra? Who goes there?'

Marjorie began to unbend. At least he had not taken the liberty of calling her Marjorie. She didn't say she had never been there but she had plenty to say about its potential, and how things might be organised.

Molly again interrupted. 'Mr Proctor is a very keen bird-watcher. He told us about the migrating birds. He has lived on Fundador for many years. I'm sure he would be helpful.'

Marjorie gave her a repressive glance. 'Mr Proctor is a quiet man, in no way an organiser - '

'He found the history book remember,' said Molly loyally.

Mr Grant looked confused, whilst making a mental note of the name Proctor.

Once at the dock, Mr Grant organised someone to carry their luggage on board. He asked about a cabin for them, and ejected an amorous couple from the only one available. Marjorie and Molly were most grateful. They stretched out on their bunks and were soon asleep. They didn't notice the rough seas and woke just in time to tidy up and be on deck to see Fundador coming into view. They felt as if a load had been taken off their shoulders.

'You know, Molly, I think we may never leave the island again,' said Marjorie.

'No,' agreed Molly. 'It really is home.'

As they neared land they were surprised to see bunting and flags on the dockside, which was bustling with people. Some fishing boats were decorated and Molly pointed out a Union Jack on the Customs House. 'Union Flag,' said Marjorie, 'That's what they call it nowadays.'

'It will always be Jack to me,' said Molly firmly. 'They can change what they like, it will always be the same on Fundador.'

'In our lifetime anyway,' said Marjorie.

Mr Grant appeared at the rail. 'What's going on? Do you know?'

'It must be a public holiday,' said Molly.

'Probably a Saint's Day,' said Marjorie. 'They're very keen on saints.' And to Molly 'Come along. The gangway is in place and we don't want to hang about. I see Amos has the taxi waiting - I thought he might forget. He's decorated it again - any excuse - '

'After you, ladies,' said Mr Grant, and they all made their way down the gangway.

On reaching the bottom Marjorie was pleased and surprised to be greeted by the Governor and his wife. 'Welcome home Mrs Bryce - Mrs Jessop. Come this way - ' and the Governor led them to a small space with a red, white and blue canopy over it, where the Chief Minister, Mr Ortego, together with Mr Enrico and Mr Branco were standing looking very formal in their city suits. From a table in front of him Mr Ortego took up a large gold-coloured key. The velvet cushion it had lain on reminded Molly of the Bournemouth Register Office and their golden wedding rings - guiltily she felt hers. Should they have given them back? It was all a long time ago.

'Mrs Bryce, My Lady, we wish to present to you the Freedom of Fundador and Assandra,' and he handed the key reverentially to Marjorie.

Able as ever to rise to the occasion, Marjorie said: 'Chief Minister, I thank you and your colleagues for the honour you have bestowed upon me. I hope that I will always justify your faith in me. My sister and I - '

'Queen of Fundador?' whispered the Governor's wife.

'Queen of Fundador,' her husband agreed, and they smiled at each other.

Mr Grant watched all this with some surprise. She wasn't kidding when she said she had influence.

After this little ceremony the local band played a selection from Gilbert and Sullivan. 'Rather appropriate,' the Governor's wife said, and again His Excellency agreed.

Miss Genova now greeted Molly warmly and said she must come to tea, they both must come to tea, very soon, and tell her all about it. Amos ran forward, nearly banging heads with Mr Proctor, as they both bowed and said 'Welcome home.'

Mr Proctor was his usual modest self. It had never entered his head to wonder why, when he had made the discovery which had solved the Assandra problem, Mrs Bryce alone should be covered with glory. His action had been minuted in the House of Representative records as 'It was ascertained that Assandra belonged to Fundador ...' Mr Proctor had paid his fine to the library, and taken out a book on Ancient Rome. Now he said to Molly, 'You must allow me to refresh you with coffee after next Sunday's service, dear lady.' Molly blushed and said she would love that.

'Come along,' said Marjorie, 'this is no time for idle chatter.'

Amos had put the luggage in the front of the taxi and the ladies got into the back, amid much cheering and waving, which Marjorie acknowledged in regal fashion. Then they made their way slowly to the Villa Marmol, not because of crowds of well-wishers, but because of the state of Amos' taxi. Despite one or two sharp reports from the exhaust they made it and Matty was on the doorstep to meet them, chanting 'Home is Mom - Big Mom and Little Mom - good Moms - '

'She's really learning English at last,' said Marjorie. Then slowly to Matty, 'Yes, here we are, and we need a cup of tea. TEA. And biscuits. Bourbon biscuits.'

'Tea and burby biccies,' Matty repeated happily, and went off to the kitchen.

'What is the freedom of Fundador and Assandra?' Molly asked, as they settled themselves over the tea table.

'I don't really know. There's no public transport for me to travel on free and I certainly don't want to go to Assandra. I think it's just another kind of medal.'

Looking at the framed certificates from The League Against Cruel Sports and the Anti-Vivisection League, the medal from the RSPCA, and the citation for the MBE, Molly suddenly thought of their parents. Life here was so full she seldom thought of them these days. She said to Marjorie, 'Mother and Father would have been so proud of you,' and Marjorie nodded her head complacently.

In silence for a moment, Molly pondered the transformation of their lives.

'And it's all because we came to Fundador,' said Molly in wonderment. 'So it really all happened because of them. They introduced us to Fundador.'

'So they did, Molly.'

'They always knew what was right for us.'

Secretly Marjorie thought that it was she who had always known what was right for all of them, but she could afford to be generous.

'They did,' she agreed. And she poured from the silver teapot into the porcelain cups.